JERRY

ON THE LINE

by Brenda Seabrooke

To Julie—
Happy reading &
Soccer playing!
Brenda Seabrooke
4-6-92

PUFFIN BOOKS

To my son Kevin—a once, present, and always hero

PUFFIN BOOKS
Published by the Penguin Group
Viking Penguin, a division of Penguin Books USA Inc.,
375 Hudson Street, New York, New York 10014, U.S.A.
Penguin Books Ltd, 27 Wrights Lane, London W8 5TZ, England
Penguin Books Australia Ltd, Ringwood, Victoria, Australia
Penguin Books Canada Ltd, 10 Alcorn Avenue, Toronto, Ontario, Canada M4V 3B2
Penguin Books (N.Z.) Ltd, 182–190 Wairau Road, Auckland 10, New Zealand

Penguin Books Ltd, Registered Offices: Harmondsworth, Middlesex, England

First published in the United States of America by
Bradbury Press, an affiliate of Macmillan, Inc., 1990
Published in Puffin Books, 1992
1   3   5   7   9   10   8   6   4   2
Copyright © Brenda Seabrooke, 1990
All rights reserved

LIBRARY OF CONGRESS CATALOGING-IN-PUBLICATION DATA
Seabrooke, Brenda.
Jerry on the line / by Brenda Seabrooke.   p.   cm.
Summary: Fourth grader Jerry, latchkey kid and aspiring soccer
star, starts an unusual friendship with a younger latchkey kid when
she calls his number by accident.
ISBN 0-14-034868-9
[1. Latchkey children—Fiction.   2. Soccer—Fiction.
3. Friendship—Fiction.]   I. Title.
PZ7.S4376Jc   1992   [Fic]—dc20   91-29549

Printed in the United States of America
Set in Baskerville

Jerry turned and saw a little girl standing on the sidewalk.

Then Tank took the ball out. He passed it to his lieutenant, but Jerry darted by and snagged it again. As he dribbled downfield in a zigzag pattern, he came closer to the little girl. He thought she was about the size of a second grader. She was watching the game.

Someone zipped the ball away from Jerry. Jerry's attention snapped back to the game. He tore out in pursuit, caught up, and kicked out before the other player could defend the ball. Ricky was there to pick it up and take it to the goal.

Jerry looked back at the kid. It couldn't be, he thought. It had to be a coincidence. Sherita wouldn't have come to his playground . . . or would she?

"Seabrooke's snappy play-by-play soccer descriptions charge through the text. . . . Readers will want to tag along as Jerry resolves his vexing situations and learns to temper his treasured independence with sound judgement."

—*Booklist*

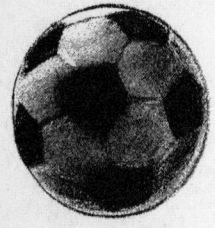

CHAPTER 1

"Beat'cha to the playground," Ricky said.

"Oh, yeah?" Jerry yelled over his shoulder as he jumped off the last two steps of Van Vickle Elementary. "This is gonna be a soccer day."

"You better get going then," Joel said. He was Jerry's best friend and always on his side. "Beat Tank."

Jerry was already running. He spotted a Pepsi can in the alley ahead and sped toward it. He gave it a mighty thwack with his foot. The can spun through the air. Jerry raced after it.

He could almost hear the announcer's voice.

"The first kick of the afternoon by the fabulous JJ Johnson, soccer fans, and it is a beaut!"

Jerry liked to run after being cooped up in the fourth grade all day. It felt good to limber up and stretch his legs. Also, practicing with the can was good for his soccer game. Jerry lived for soccer. He wanted to be a soccer star when he grew up. Everybody knew that sport stars were heroes. He planned to be a soccer star and a hero, too, and he needed all the soccer practice he could get.

Jerry had another reason for racing through the alleys. He had to get home in a hurry. Before he could go to the playground every day, he had to go home and check in with his mother by phone. It was a rule. So instead of walking with his friends, he took a shortcut. He could get home sooner running through the alleys. Then he could get to the playground faster, before Tank or any of Tank's friends. The unwritten rule of the playground was that the first kid there got to choose the game for the day. Jerry wanted to be first so he could choose soccer. The spring soccer season was only a few months away, and he wouldn't be able to practice after the snow fell.

The can skimmed ahead of Jerry. He caught up to it and kicked it hard, straight up the middle of the alley. A real bomb. A bullet. If he'd been on the soccer field, he bet it would have gone right between the goalie's legs.

Jerry reached the last alley. He tried to cover it with one kick. He let his momentum carry him as he came up on the can. Without breaking stride, he swung his left foot. *Whambo!* The can shot forward with Jerry right behind.

He was going to make it. The can hit the ground halfway down the alley but that was okay. It would roll the rest of the way unless something blocked it, something like that old bicycle tire right in the can's path. Jerry put on a burst of speed. He reached the tire an instant before the can did and whipped the tire out of the way. The can rolled by.

Saved in the nick of time by Jerry Johnson. The crowd went wild. The announcers gave up trying to be heard as the crowd roared, "JJ! JJ! JJ!"

The can rolled to a stop at the edge of the sidewalk. Jerry crossed the street and went in the door of his apartment building. He was almost two blocks ahead of his friends from school. Ricky and Abe were probably in the lead but that was okay. He knew he could beat them to the playground. It was Tank he really had to beat. Tank always chose football. But even Tank had to go home first.

Jerry needed to play soccer. He had to play soccer. He sprinted up the stairway to his floor and down the hall. He counted off the doors. Almost there. He skidded to a stop in front of his door. He could hear the telephone ringing inside.

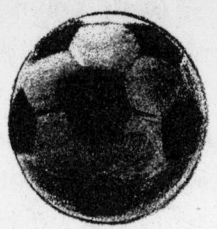

CHAPTER 2

Jerry pulled out his door key. He loved coming home by himself and unlocking the door with his own key. He could hear the phone inside still ringing.

"I'm coming," he yelled through the door. But just as he slid the key into the lock, the ringing stopped. Jerry wondered who had called. His mother wouldn't call this early.

Jerry liked being a latchkey kid. He was glad his parents trusted him with his own key. They were saving to buy a house and maybe a trucking rig for his father. His mother had gone back to work last summer so they could hurry things along. They were able to save even more because they didn't have to pay for a sitter for Jerry.

Jerry would never forget the day his parents had given him his key. They'd made it into a celebration. His dad had brought home Chinese carryout and a chocolate cake from the bakery for dessert. Then they had given him a box wrapped in shiny silver paper tied with a silver ribbon. Inside, on a bed of cotton, had been a key to their apartment door. It was on a chain. As Jerry had proudly hung it around his neck, his dad had said, "Now you can help us save for the new house."

Most of Jerry's friends were latchkey kids, too. Only David's mother stayed at home, but he had a new baby brother. David always told people he would be a latchkey kid soon.

Jerry slipped the chain over his head and stuffed the key back under his shirt. Scooter and John wore their keys on their belts with a bunch of other old keys they'd found in a trash dump. Their keys jangled when they walked and made them feel important. Jerry didn't want to carry more than one key. The weight would slow him down.

Sometimes at school he wore the key outside

his shirt to impress a new kid or a teacher. A latchkey kid was somebody special, Jerry thought, somebody who knew how to take care of himself.

Jerry liked coming home to an empty apartment. He pretended he was grown up and coming home from his job to his own place where nobody could see anything he did. He could put his feet on the coffee table in front of the sofa and drink his milk without anybody to see his milk moustache and tell him to use a napkin. Or he could lick the plate his cake had been on and nobody was there to tell him to mind his manners.

But there were rules. His parents were very strict about the rules. They were posted on the door of the refrigerator, held up by the four magnets shaped like soccer balls that he had given his mother for Christmas to hold recipes and things.

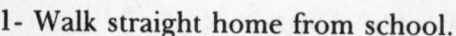

1- Walk straight home from school.
2- Don't bring anybody home with you.
3- Don't open the door for anybody.
4- Keep the door locked at all times.
5- Wait for Mom's call.
6- Don't call her office except in an emergency.

Jerry's mother called every day at the same time to see that he had gotten home safely. She was a receptionist at a clinic. He wasn't supposed to call her there because personal calls were only for emergencies. So far there hadn't been an emergency. When his dad was home the rules didn't apply, because then Jerry wasn't a latchkey kid, although he was allowed to keep his key. But his dad was a trucker and away a lot.

Jerry made a quick sandwich while he waited for his mother's call. He mashed up a banana with peanut butter and spread it on two slices of bread. The banana was mushy, the way he liked it because when he mixed it with crunchy peanut butter, the gooey goop spread more easily. He took a big bite and poured a glass of milk while he chewed.

He wished his mom would hurry and call. Then he could have his snack on the run and be the first kid on the playground. Every day as he waited for her call, it seemed like he was waiting for next year.

Jerry was halfway through his sandwich and milk when the phone finally rang. He pounced on it in midring.

"Hello, Mom?"

"Yes, Jerry, it's me. Did you have a good day?"

Jerry thought his mother always sounded so businesslike when she called from the clinic. "Yeah. It was okay. About like usual." Then he remembered he had something to tell her. "I got a B+ on my spelling test."

"That's good. Did you bring the test home?"

"Um-hum." Jerry took another bite of sandwich.

"Well, you'll have to study the ones you missed. Next time, try for an A."

"Um-hum."

"Jerry, don't talk with your mouth full."

Jerry grinned. She couldn't see him but she could hear him. You couldn't fool mothers. He swallowed loudly. "Okay, Mom."

She laughed. "Well, all right, Jerry. Have fun but remember the rules."

Jerry eyed the playground rules. They were posted below the apartment rules. They were held up by four more soccer ball magnets that Jerry had given his father for his birthday in case he ever wanted to post anything on the fridge.

1- No detours. Go straight to the playground.
2- There must be at least 5 other kids on the playground.
3- Do not leave the playground until you are ready to come home.
4- You must be home 15 minutes before 5.
5- Walk home in a group.
6- No detours. Come straight home.

Underneath these rules there was a list of emergency numbers held up by four backup soccer magnets that Jerry had given his mother in case some of the others broke or got lost.

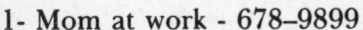

1- Mom at work - 678–9899
2- police - 222–1231
3- fire dept. - 222–7788
4- apartment super - 789–9007
5- Dr. Naggi - 678–4678
6- Grandpa and Gram - 788–5565
7- David's mom - 789–0076
8- ARO Trucking - 678–4421

There was no way he could forget all those rules and regulations, Jerry thought.

"Okay, Mom. See you tonight."

Jerry hung up the phone and finished his milk. He wiped his mouth on his sleeve, scooped up his soccer ball from the floor of the hall closet, and was turning to go when the phone rang again. Jerry turned around to answer it. His mother must have forgotten something.

CHAPTER 3

"Hello, Mom?" Jerry said.

"Hello," said a tiny voice. It wasn't his mother.

When the voice didn't speak, Jerry said again, "Hello? Who are you calling?"

"Hello? Who is this?" said the little voice.

"Jerry." He knew he wasn't supposed to give his name over the phone. He didn't give his last name. Nobody would know who Jerry was. There could be millions of Jerrys in the city. Anyway, it was probably the little sister or brother of one of his friends.

"Hi, Jerry," the tiny voice piped with enthusiasm, as if it, whoever it was, had known Jerry forever.

"Who are you calling?" he asked.

"I'm calling you," said the little voice.

"But who are you?"

"I'm Sherita."

Jerry couldn't remember anybody named Sherita. "Are you somebody's sister?"

"No, I don't have any brothers or sisters. Do you?"

"No. Listen, if you're not somebody's sister, how'd you get this number?"

"I made it up." She giggled.

"How?" Jerry asked.

"It was easy. I just wrote down a bunch of numbers and then I dialed them."

"But why?"

"I wanted somebody to talk to."

"But you don't know me."

"Now I do."

Jerry decided not to argue with her. "Never mind," he said. "It's been nice talking to you, Sherita, but I've got to—"

"Jerry," Sherita interrupted quickly, "do you know anything about animals?"

"Well, a little. I'm in the fourth grade. And I've

been to the zoo. But I'm going to be la—"

"I'm in the second grade," Sherita interrupted again. "I went to the zoo once but it was a long time ago when I was little. I was scared of the bears."

"The bears can't hurt you," Jerry told her. "They are penned in. You're safe at the zoo. Now I've—"

"They might get out and follow me home," she said.

"No, they won't. The zookeepers won't let them," Jerry assured her.

"They might," she insisted.

"Not if you keep your door locked. Bears can't open locked doors."

"You don't know that."

"Yes, I do. Who ever heard of a bear opening a door? They've got better things to do. Like me. I've—"

"Like what?"

Jerry tried to think. What do bears do? "Well, they look for beehives. You don't have a beehive in your apartment, do you?"

"Noooo."

"There." Jerry was triumphant. He'd won the

argument. "Bears won't bother you if you don't have a beehive."

"You don't know that."

"Yes, I do."

"Uh-uh."

Jerry slumped against the wall. You couldn't win an argument with this kid even when you were right. How was he ever going to get off the phone? Jerry knew that he could just hang up and leave. But she sounded so tiny. He couldn't be mean to her. And his parents had taught him to be polite on the telephone. What could he do? He had to get off the phone or he would be late to the playground. He decided to change the subject to get her mind off bears.

"What kind of animals do you like?" he asked.

"I don't know. I haven't seen many animals."

She had just said she'd been to the zoo. What a dumb kid. But he didn't want to mention the zoo. She might start talking about bears again. "There must be some animals you like."

"Well, I like cats. Do you?"

"Sure." Jerry was glad that his ploy had worked. Now maybe he could get her to hang up. "Listen, Sherita, I've got to—"

But before he finished his sentence, she asked another question. "Do you know how many humps a camel has?"

Jerry tried to picture a camel. "Sure. A camel has two humps." He paused. "No, one. Well, some camels have one and some have two."

"That's not right. Camels have to have the same number of humps. One or two. Which is it?"

"Just what I said. Sometimes they have one hump and sometimes two."

"You don't know much," Sherita said.

"Just a minute, Sherita. I don't have time to argue about camels. I'm late for my soccer game. Anyway, this is a dumb conversation."

"It's not dumb. I have to know. It's for school. I have to answer some questions about animals. We saw a video but now I can't 'member how many humps camels have. I need help."

"Why are you bothering me about it? Ask somebody else," Jerry said. He was impatient to be off.

"I don't know anybody else," she said.

"You could ask your mother."

"I can't call her at work 'less it's a 'mergency. And she might not know."

"Don't you have a sitter?"

"No. I stay by myself."

"I'm a latchkey kid, too," Jerry said with pride.

"Do you like coming home when nobody's there?" she whispered.

"Sure," Jerry said. "It makes me feel grown up."

"Oh."

There was a long pause. Jerry was about to say good-bye when she said, "It makes me feel lonesome. That's why I call people up. I want somebody to talk to."

"That makes sense," Jerry said. That was what he would do if he were lonesome. But he had Joel and David and the rest of his gang to call.

"What about people in your class?" he suggested. "Can't you call some of them?"

"I don't know their numbers. I don't know anybody outside of school."

Jerry sighed. Surely she knew somebody in the whole world. "There must be somebody you can call, a neighbor maybe."

"No, I don't know anybody. But now I know you."

Jerry groaned. He didn't believe there was

nobody she could call. But he didn't want to risk getting into another argument with her. She had a way of winning.

Sherita asked again. "Well, do you know how many humps a camel has?"

"I'm thinking," Jerry told her. "You ask too many questions."

"But I have to ask questions if I don't know the answers. My teacher, Miss White, says we should ask questions to find out things."

Jerry brightened. He knew what to tell her now. Mrs. Brent always told his class to look things up. "You can look up *camel* in the encyclopedia. There will be a picture and you can count the humps. There might even be three humps."

"I don't have a 'cyclopedia. Do you?"

"Well, yes, but . . ."

"Look it up for me, please, Jerry," she said.

"Can't you go to the library and look it up?"

"I'm not allowed to leave the apartment," Sherita said.

"You could look it up at school tomorrow," Jerry suggested.

"I have to turn in my homework first thing in the morning."

"Hold on," Jerry said with resignation. He was

going to get this over with in a hurry.

He ran to the bookcase and got out the *C* volume of the encyclopedia. He flipped the pages as fast as he could, overshot *camel,* and had to back up. At last he found it.

"I was right," he told Sherita. "Sometimes camels have two humps, the ones that live in China or Mongolia, and if they live in Africa or western Asia they have one hump."

There was a silence. Then Sherita said, "How should I answer the question? There's only room for one answer on the line."

Jerry gritted his teeth. He was never going to get to the playground in time. "The answer doesn't have to be on the line."

"Miss White says it does. She gets onto us if we aren't neat."

"Look, Sherita, get a ruler and make a nice straight line under the line for the answer. Then write down that some camels have one hump and some have two."

"Are you sure?"

Jerry felt like pulling his hair out. "Of course, I'm sure. I'm looking at the answer right here in the encyclopedia. Don't you believe the encyclopedia?"

"The 'cyclopedia doesn't have to answer Miss White."

Jerry groaned. "Sherita, Miss White gets her questions from books like the encyclopedia."

"How do you know?"

"Because I know. I gotta go now, Sherita."

"Okay, Jerry. Can I call you up sometimes?"

"Yeah, sometimes. Now I gotta go. I'm late."

"You can call me, too. Write down my number. It's 423–2494."

Jerry wasn't going to write down her number. He couldn't think of a single reason for ever calling Sherita.

"Did you write it down?" she asked.

"Um-hum." Jerry didn't bother to hide his impatience now.

"Well, read it back to me," Sherita demanded.

"Uh . . ."

"I knew you didn't. This time, do it. It's 423–2494."

Jerry did it, just to get her out of his hair. He wrote the number on his mother's pad by the phone. Then he drew a circle around it and made x's along the circle. It looked like a tiny barbed-wire fence.

"Okay, I did it." He read the number back to

her. He knew that was the one number in the world that he would never call. "Now I gotta go. Good-bye."

Jerry hung up the phone and grabbed his soccer ball even though he knew he was too late to get to the playground first. Tank would be there for sure and that meant Jerry would have to play football instead of soccer.

"Jeeps," he said as he closed the door behind him.

CHAPTER 4

Jerry wasn't the last at the playground but he wasn't first and that was what counted. He was glad that Tank wasn't first. Tank was built like a tank and football was his game. There were always a couple of boys hanging around him. Everybody called them Tank's army.

Jerry and his friends didn't like to play football against Tank and his army. Abe didn't mind it but he preferred basketball. Scooter liked baseball. John and Ricky liked everything but football with Tank. Joel always chose soccer because he was Jerry's best friend.

The playground wasn't officially a playground. It was only a vacant lot between two tall buildings. It didn't have slides or swings or any kind of equipment, but it was better than no playground. Two poles with hoops nailed to them served as basketball nets. The poles were set at right angles to each other instead of at each end of the lot so that the rules had to be bent for a basketball game. There were no lines marking a soccer or football field, and pieces of trash marked the goals.

When Jerry arrived the game had already been decided. Abe had been the first on the playground so the game for the day was basketball.

Joel was always the referee. He was always picking up bugs and things to take home and look at under his microscope. Sometimes he even picked them up in the middle of a game. But nobody else wanted to be referee.

"Okay, sports fiends, let's play ball," Joel said.

Abe and Tank got ready to jump for the ball. They were about the same height, but Abe had longer arms. Joel blew his whistle and threw the ball up in the air. Tank and Abe jumped at the same time. Abe slapped the ball to David. The game was on.

David sank the first shot before Tank's army had warmed up. Tank threw the ball to one of his lieutenants who took it out and threw it right back to Tank.

Half of the army blocked Abe, while the other half blocked David as Tank dribbled toward the basket. Jerry and the other boys were free to dart around and try to steal the ball.

Tank wasn't good at basketball (or any game except football) but he still wanted to be the star. He shot an air ball. Jerry was right under the hoop waiting for it. Tank never learned.

Jerry's team passed the ball around. Ricky sent it back to Jerry on the way to the basket. David took Jerry's pass on the outside and then, before the army knew it was coming, he bounce passed it to Abe under the basket. Abe turned and made a backhanded lay-up.

Tank jerked his head and the same lieutenant took the ball out. He threw it in to Tank. The army again tried to keep Abe and David away from Tank. Jerry, with no one on him, stole the ball from Tank and passed to Abe. The army swarmed around him. Abe passed it to David in shooting range and he swished it.

Jerry knew Tank was frustrated because he had

lost the ball twice. He was careful not to get close enough for a collision. But Abe was not so lucky. Tank dribbled under his team's basket with Abe right on him. Then Tank lunged and Abe went down.

Joel's whistle shrilled. "Foul on Tank," he said.

"He ran into me," Tank argued. "I'm the one with the ball. He fouled me."

"I'm the one with the whistle, Tank. Foul on you." Joel blew his whistle again and handed the ball to Jerry.

Jerry threw it in to John. He took it down to the hoop. John passed it back to Jerry there and he buried it.

One of Tank's lieutenants finally managed to get the ball away from Tank and make a basket. Jerry was glad. He didn't like to see a team skunked, even if it was Tank's team.

"What made you so late?" Joel asked Jerry as they were walking home.

"I had a phone call," Jerry said.

"I thought maybe you weren't coming. You've been first every day this month. It was a record."

Jerry winced at that. He didn't need to be reminded that he had missed a day of soccer.

Jerry had known he was born to play soccer since he was four and his dad took him to his first soccer match. He'd loved all the action and excitement of the game just as his dad did. He'd wanted to jump right on the field and kick the ball down to the goal. It was the greatest game in the world.

They'd play soccer tomorrow, Jerry knew, if that kid didn't call him again. Sherita. It was her fault he was late. Why did she have to make up his number out of all the zillions of telephone numbers in the city?

CHAPTER 5

"Soccer fans," the announcer shouted over the din, "you have never seen anything like what we have just witnessed today in the Arenacade. JJ has broken the all-time record of goals scored by one player in a single game! This has been an unbelievable afternoon in the annals of soccer. Fantastic! Stupendous!"

The crowd was on its feet, roaring its approval. "JJ! JJ! JJ!"

Jerry could still hear the echo of the shouts as he unlocked his apartment door after school the next day. It was his favorite sound.

He was chewing the last bite of a peanut butter and mustard sandwich when his mother called.

"Hi, Jerry."

"Everything's okay, Mom. Gotta go," he said.

"What's your hurry?"

"You know, Mom. If I get to the playground first, I get to play soccer."

"I know, Jerry. I'm only teasing."

"Awww, Mom."

"I know you're in a rush, but can you spare a second and please take the casserole for tonight out of the refrigerator for me? It's on the bottom shelf wrapped in foil. Put it in the oven and turn it on bake. The temperature is already set."

"Yeah, Mom, okay." Jerry dashed to the fridge and found the casserole.

"All done," he reported.

"Thanks, Jerry. See you tonight."

"Bye, Mom," he said into the phone. Now to get out of here before that little kid called. He was still wearing his jacket. All he had to do was grab his soccer ball and . . .

The phone rang. Jerry hesitated. He didn't want to answer it. But it might be his mom calling back. Or his dad calling from somewhere. It could be his grandmother or Aunt Ruth or . . . He picked up the phone.

"Hello?"

"Hi, Jerry. This is Sherita. What are you doing?"

Oh no! Jerry almost yelled it into the phone. But before he could answer, she was talking again so fast he had to listen carefully to understand her. "You said I could call, 'member? Do you know how to make a camel out of playclay?"

"A what? A camel? No, I—"

"I have to make an animal for my science project. Did you ever have to do that?"

"No. Sherita, I have to go to—"

Sherita interrupted. "I tried to make a camel like we talked about yesterday. One with two humps. But it looks like a dog with an elephant on its back."

Jerry had to laugh at her description. "Once I made an elephant in art class. It looked like a cat with a string hanging off its nose."

Sherita giggled. "It's hard to make things out of playclay if you're not very good at it. I'm not very good."

"Me neither. Why do you have to make a camel? That's hard."

"Everybody in the class has to make an animal. Then we have to write a report about it. I picked camels on account of you know a lot about them."

"No, I don't," Jerry protested quickly.

"But you could look it up for me."

"But I can't make it for you."

"That's true. What can I do? I'll get a bad grade if I turn in a camel that looks like a dog. And everybody will laugh at me. . . ." Her voice trailed off.

Jerry sighed. He pictured her sniffling into the phone. She was probably a skinny little kid with her top front teeth missing, big eyes, and tiny braids with bunny barrettes on the ends. She had that kind of voice. He'd better make short work of her problem so he could be on his way. This would be a snap today.

"You'll have to make an easier animal like a snake or something," he told her.

"Jimmy is doing a snake."

Jerry stood on his left foot. "How about a fish?"

"Harry is doing a fish."

"Can't you do it, too?"

"No. Miss White says everybody has to do a different one."

Seals and pandas had already been picked.

Jerry tried to think. What would be easy for a little kid to make? A lion? A giraffe? They were hard. Everything he could think of was either too hard or somebody else was doing it. He didn't want to mention bears. "What about penguins?"

"Mark is doing them."

"Did anybody choose turtles? They're pretty easy."

"Noooo, I don't think anybody did."

Jerry stood on his right foot, ready to run. "Well, then, do a turtle."

"Okay."

Jerry was relieved that he had solved her problem for today. Now he could hang up. He might still get to the playground first. "I gotta go now—" he began.

"Wait, Jerry. What color are turtles?"

"Different colors."

"What colors?" she persisted.

"Jeeps." Jerry tried to think of turtle colors. "Brown. Gray. Green. Yellow spotted. I don't know. Get a book at the library and find out. You'll have to do that anyway for your report."

There was a long pause. Jerry was about to hang up when she said, "I thought you could tell me about turtles."

"I don't know much about turtles, Sherita. Anyway, you're supposed to do the work. Not me."

"I'll try," Sherita said, but Jerry could hear the doubt in her voice.

"You do that. Now I gotta go. Bye."

"Bye, Jerry. Thank you."

Click. Jerry put the receiver down, picked up his soccer ball and was out the door in one continuous motion. He felt a twinge of guilt for giving Sherita the brush-off like that. He suspected he could have helped her, but he had to get to the playground.

Jerry ran as fast as he could but he was fifth. Scooter and John were first.

"We get to choose," Scooter said.

"Yeah," John echoed.

Jerry hoped they would choose soccer. "Come on, guys, let's play soccer."

"We've played soccer for a whole month," Scooter said.

"Except yesterday," Joel reminded them.

"Yeah. That was fun," said John. "Let's do it again."

"Okay with me." Abe grinned.

Tank and his army didn't look happy about the

choice. Jerry and Joel didn't either, but they didn't want to be classed with Tank.

"Okay," they both agreed.

Basketball was better than football with Tank. Anything was.

"You've been late twice now," Joel said to Jerry as they were walking home.

"Yeah, what's happening?" Abe asked.

"I get these calls." Jerry didn't want to explain about Sherita, not even to Joel. He didn't want anybody to know that a girl, a second-grade girl, had made him late to the playground. "How do you get rid of somebody on the phone?" he asked the group.

"Nobody ever calls me," said Scooter.

"Me neither," said John. " 'Cept my grandmother."

"My cousin called me once," Ricky told them. "I didn't want to talk to her but my mother made me 'cause she was moving to Los Angeles. She told me she's going to be a movie star." He snorted. "She's so ugly, she'd scare Godzilla."

"I got a cousin like that," David said. "She wants to be a policeman. She'll scare the crooks to death."

"You can pretend to be the wrong number,"

Joel said, answering Jerry's question.

"Yeah!" It was brilliant. Jerry wondered why he hadn't thought of it. Next time Sherita called, he'd pretend to be a wrong number.

Jerry's mother was setting the table in the kitchen as he let himself into the apartment. He sniffed. Tuna casserole. He should have guessed. It had sour cream and mushrooms and other yucky stuff that Jerry didn't want to know about. He usually pretended it was a peanut butter and banana sandwich and swallowed it after chewing as little as possible.

Jerry leaned against the kitchen counter and took a gulp of cold milk.

"How was your day?" his mother asked.

"It was okay." As okay as a day without soccer could be. As okay as a day with a phone call from Sherita could be.

"Mom, what do you do when people call and you don't want to talk to them?"

"People you know, Jerry, or strangers?"

Jerry thought for a minute. He didn't *really know* Sherita. "Strangers, I guess."

His mother frowned. "Have you been getting crank calls?"

"No, Mom." Sherita was a phone freak but not a crank.

"Well, if you do, hang up immediately."

"Oh, I will," Jerry promised. "You can bet I will."

CHAPTER 6

Today Jerry was sure he would be first on the playground. He had a plan. When the phone rang, he was ready.

"Hi, Jerry—" Sherita began.

Jerry took a deep breath and interrupted. "This is Geraldine, not Jerry," he said in a high voice that he hoped sounded like a girl.

"But—"

"You have the wrong number, little girl." Jerry hung up and lunged for the door, but immediately the phone rang again.

"Hi, Jerry, this is—"

"Little girl, you have the wrong number," he said in a falsetto voice.

He hung up and leaped for the door but again the phone rang. Sherita must be the world's fastest dialer, he thought. For two cents he wouldn't answer, but it might be his mother.

"Hi, Jerry—"

"Stop bothering me, you phone freak." Jerry forgot to use the high voice, but he knew he wasn't fooling Sherita.

"This is Sherita." She continued the conversation as though he hadn't spoken.

Jerry slumped by the phone. It was no use. He bet she'd keep calling him all afternoon. He might as well listen to her and get it over with.

"I made the turtle just like you told me and guess what happened?"

Jerry didn't want to know. He didn't want to talk to Sherita. He didn't want to help her with her science project.

He didn't say anything.

"Guess."

There was a long pause. Then Sherita said, "You'll never guess what happened, Jerry. One side of the turtle's shell caved in. It just fell in. Why do you suppose that happened?"

Jerry could think of several reasons. But he didn't want to get involved. Sherita was the most persistent kid he knew. It seemed that the only way to get rid of her was to change his telephone number or be rude. He knew his parents wouldn't change the number. He would have to be rude. It was the only way. He had to play soccer. He took a deep breath.

"I have to go now." He hung up without saying good-bye or even giving Sherita a chance to say good-bye. If he had, she would have kept on talking until tomorrow.

He grabbed his soccer ball and ran out of the apartment. As the door slammed he heard the phone ring again, but he was already on his way.

As he ran, Jerry felt both happy and guilty. He was happy because he hadn't been stuck on the phone a long time. Today he would be first at the playground.

Still, he felt guilty because he had hung up on Sherita. She was only a little kid. She didn't have anybody to help her with her project. But it was a choice between what she wanted and what he wanted. Jerry chose soccer.

Jerry's feet skimmed over the sidewalk as though he had grown wings where his little toes were. Soon, he forgot all about Sherita. His big toes tingled with anticipation as he thought about dribbling the soccer ball down the whole length of the playground. This was going to be his day.

Jerry turned the corner and stopped short. Tank was in the middle of the playground tossing his football high in the air and running underneath to catch it.

It wasn't possible. Jerry had run home faster than ever, cut short his conversation with Sherita, and sped to the playground. Tank couldn't move fast enough to beat him even though he lived closer than Jerry did.

"How'd you get here so fast?" he demanded.

Tank grinned. "Maybe I've been practicing my running. Football players have to run, too. It's gonna be football today."

"I can see that." Jerry threw his soccer ball down. He felt miserable and mad at the same time.

The soccer ball bounced high with the force of Jerry's throw and continued bouncing again and again. Jerry ran behind it and kicked it with fast, furious kicks all around the playground. He was out of breath when the rest of the gang arrived.

They looked at Jerry kicking the soccer ball and

at Tank throwing the football up over his head.

"Which is it?" Abe asked.

"Football," Tank gloated. His army smirked.

One reason that Jerry didn't like to play football was that he had to carry the ball a lot because he was fast. Abe had to carry it, too, because he was tall and could catch better than anybody else. It took all of the army to get Abe down, but it only took one to tackle Jerry. Everybody Tank tackled always went down. Everybody on Jerry's team tried not to get tackled by Tank.

Joel refereed, as usual. If Tank fell on him, it would kill him or break his glasses. He pulled out the whistle he wore on a string with his latchkey and blew it. "Okay, guys. Huddle."

Both teams went into a huddle even though only one was supposed to. Tank and the army won the toss so they had to huddle to decide on a play. Jerry's team had to huddle to decide what they thought Tank was going to do and what they would do about it.

"I think they'll give the ball to Tank right away," Ricky said. "They haven't played football in a long time and you know how Tank likes to hog the ball."

"All right, guys, everybody go after Tank," Abe said. "But keep your eyes on the rest of the army."

Joel blew his whistle and the two teams lined up. Tank favored an H formation he'd made up himself.

Tank carried the ball on the first play and Jerry's team piled on him, all except Abe who was covering the army.

But Tank's team made a touchdown before Jerry's team ever got the ball. Jerry tackled Tank once by himself and got dragged ten feet before John helped him.

Abe was the quarterback. After the snap, he handed off to Jerry, who almost got free. If he had, it would have been a touchdown. Ricky carried the ball on the next play and got to the end of the playground, tying the game.

Next time around, Abe again gave the ball to Jerry. Tank was waiting for him. Jerry tried to veer to the left but Tank pounced on him in a flying leap. Jerry went down with a thud on his left knee. Most of the army piled with enthusiasm on top of Tank.

Joel pulled them off, blew his whistle, and shouted, "Unnecessary roughness. Ten yard penalty."

41

Jerry got up stiffly. His left knee stung. He examined it. His jeans were ripped and they were new jeans. Almost new. He'd gotten them in September. His mother was going to be mad. She wouldn't buy him new ones until his next growth spurt. These would have to be patched.

Inside the hole a raw area of skin was rapidly turning bright red. When the red began to drip, Jerry decided he'd had enough football. He found his soccer ball and started home. It was against his parents' rules for him to walk home alone from the playground, but he thought this was a sort of emergency.

"Quitter!" yelled one of the army.

"Quitter!" echoed another.

Jerry glared at them. "I gotta put something on my knee. It's bleeding and I might need stitches." Soccer players had to take care of their knees. His was already throbbing and stiffening.

"Better wash it real good," Joel said. "You don't want to get blood poisoning."

Blood poisoning! Jerry thought he would faint. But as he limped home the faintness went away.

When he got home, Jerry pulled off his jeans and soaked the torn part in cold water the way he'd seen his mother do. His knee looked awful and felt worse. Remembering what Joel said, he washed the dirt and gravel off his knee. It stung, but it was nothing like the antiseptic that he dabbed on next. He knew he had to do it. If his knee got infected, his mother would never let him go back to the playground.

His knee felt like it was on fire. Jerry hopped around the bathroom in silent misery, fanning his knee to stop the burning.

Suddenly there was a loud thump right under his feet. Jerry stopped hopping. It was Mrs. Murphy, who lived in the apartment directly below. She probably thought he was playing soccer again in the apartment. Jerry had tried doing it once in rainy weather when he couldn't go outside. He had only dribbled the ball around, hardly making any noise at all. But Mrs. Murphy had complained to the super of the building. Now, whenever she thought he was doing it, she thumped on the ceiling of her apartment with her broomstick.

Jerry hoped she wouldn't tell his mother. He wasn't even dribbling this time, but he didn't want to have to explain. Then his mother would find out about his knee, and she might make him stay home from the playground.

He tiptoed over to the shower and turned it on. Maybe Mrs. Murphy would hear the running water and think he was jumping to get out of his pants to take a shower. Maybe she would think he lost his balance and fell over.

Jerry found a patch in his mother's sewing box. He hoped he had time to iron it on before she got home. He had watched her do it plenty of times.

Jerry dried the knee part of his jeans with his mother's hair dryer so the patch would stick. But the hair dryer took too long. Jerry ran the hot iron over the wet part of his jeans. Then he started on the patch.

He heard his mother's key in the front door just as he got the patch ironed on. He unplugged the iron and put it back in the pantry. She wouldn't notice it was still warm.

The door was opening. Jerry stuck the ironing board back in the closet. He grabbed his warm pants and ran to his room. Now all he had to do was find another pair to put on and he was home free.

"Jerry?" his mother called. "Are you home yet?"

Jerry hopped into his other jeans and zipped them up. "Yeah, Mom. I'm in my room."

That night Jerry had trouble falling asleep. His throbbing knee reminded him of his day. Right over his bed was his favorite soccer poster, the one of Pelé. It was the last thing he saw at night before he went to sleep and the first thing he saw when he woke up in the morning. He lay in bed staring at the soccer ball Pelé was kicking. Jerry had painted it with luminous paint so it would glow in the dark. He was never afraid with the ball up there. If he woke up in the middle of the night, he could see it shining over him like a big white moon.

Jerry thought about Sherita. She probably had a nightlight because she was afraid of bears. He shouldn't have hung up on her. Look what had happened to him since. If he hadn't hung up, maybe his knee wouldn't be keeping him awake.

It wasn't only his knee. Jerry knew that his conscience was bothering him, too. He imagined Sherita in her bed crying into her pillow, one arm around her teddy bear. No, she wouldn't have a teddy bear. She was afraid of bears, he remembered. She probably had a rabbit or a kitten, a pink one with matted fur and limp ears and a bedraggled ribbon. And one eye missing. She probably called it Binky and told it all her secrets. She was probably telling it right now how that mean Jerry had hung up on her and wouldn't help her with her turtle.

The covers were heavy on Jerry's knee. He kicked off a blanket. That was better. He fell asleep and dreamed that a giant pink rabbit with soccer ball eyes was chasing him.

CHAPTER 7

"How's your knee?" Joel asked the next morning as Jerry was getting his geography book out of his desk.

"Stiff and sore. How do you know if you have blood poisoning?" Joel always knew about science things.

"You get a red line running up your leg. Do you have one?"

"I didn't this morning." Jerry thought Joel looked disappointed. "Is that all? Just a red line?"

"You'd probably have a fever, too."

"I guess I don't have it then," Jerry said.

"Pass your geography homework to the front," Mrs. Brent was saying.

Jerry flipped through his notebook, then his geography book. His homework wasn't there.

Mrs. Brent noticed him. "Is there a problem, Jerry?"

"I must have left it at home," he said. "It's not here."

"You don't have your homework, Jerry?"

"I did it, Mrs. Brent. Honest. I must've left it somewhere." Jerry started thinking. He had been working on the map of Africa when his mom had said it was bedtime. He'd closed the atlas and put it back in the bookcase. His homework was probably in the atlas. Jeeps!

"Very well, Jerry. But to help you remember next time, you may answer questions four, five, eight, and nine on page forty-five."

Math was next. Jerry had four problems wrong on his homework. Then Mrs. Brent gave the class a pop spelling quiz.

"This is not my day," he complained to Joel during lunch. Jerry stabbed his orange Jell-O. It quivered horribly. Jerry liked his food to lie still on his plate.

"You're probably growing," Joel told him.

"Huh? What's that have to do with anything?"

"My dad says that when things go wrong with kids, like they have accidents and forget things, they're growing. You been falling a lot lately?"

Jerry tried to remember. "I don't think so. Only yesterday."

"That doesn't count. You had Tank and the whole army on you. Even Godzilla would've fallen down."

Jerry stabbed his Jell-O again. "Yeah. I guess."

"Are you going to eat that Jell-O?"

"No. I lost my appetite. This stuff is the color of goldfish."

"People used to eat goldfish," Joel said as he scraped the Jell-O onto his plate.

"Don't tell my mother. She might want to cook some."

"Oh, they weren't cooked," Joel said.

Jerry stared at him. "You mean they ate raw goldfish?"

"Sure. It was all for fun. My granddad said back in the twenties people used to do all kinds of crazy things."

"Like what?"

"Like trying to see how many people can crowd

into a telephone booth," Joel said as he finished the last of the Jell-O.

"That's fun?"

"I guess you had to be there," Joel said.

"Yeah."

Jerry checked his feet in PE to see if they were growing. They looked the same size to him. His sneakers felt the same too, except maybe the left one. His left big toe seemed a lot closer to the end of his sneaker.

"Can one toe grow but not the rest of your foot?" he asked Joel on the way back to their classroom.

"I don't think so," Joel said. "I think your whole foot has to grow at the same time."

Jerry didn't fall down as he ran home, not even with his knee stiff and sore. But suddenly, a car came out of nowhere and crushed the can he was kicking. Jerry stood on the curb and watched. The car sped away, leaving the flattened can lying in the street. Jerry felt as though that can had been his pet and he wanted to take it home and bury it in his backyard. Except he didn't have one.

Jerry didn't bother to look for another can. With his luck it would get mashed by a Mack truck. Anyway, today he wanted to concentrate on getting right to the playground.

But his bad luck held. First, there weren't any bananas. Then, before he was halfway through his peanut butter and applesauce sandwich, the telephone rang for the second time. His mother had already called. He knew she wasn't calling back. But she might be. He had to answer it. The peanut butter made a huge unswallowable lump in his mouth. Jerry let the phone ring again as he rolled the lump around in his mouth. With a mighty gulp, he forced it down and answered the phone.

"Hi, Jerry, this is Sherita. We got cut off yesterday. I tried to call you back but nobody was there. Do you 'member what happened to my turtle?" Without waiting for his reply, she went on, "It went flat. It looks like somebody sat on it and the tail fell off. What can I do to fix it? I have to take it to school on Monday."

Sherita didn't seem to realize that Jerry had hung up on her the day before. It made him feel like the meanest kid in the world.

"That's no problem, Sherita. You can glue the tail back on. And this can be a flat turtle."

"Are there flat turtles, Jerry?" There was doubt

in her voice. "I never saw any pictures of flat turtles."

"Yours can be flat," Jerry said.

"But if real turtles aren't flat, I don't want my turtle to be flat."

"It's okay to make a flat turtle," Jerry insisted. He chewed his peanut butter. It felt like a lump of guilt going down his gullet. He figured it was about halfway to his stomach now. It wouldn't seem to go any further. Maybe it was stuck.

"How can I fix my turtle, Jerry?"

Maybe if he jumped up and down the lump would go down.

"Are you there, Jerry?"

"Yeah, I'm still here." Jerry jumped. Nothing happened.

"You sound funny, Jerry."

Jerry jumped up and down as he talked. "I'm okay. Listen, Sherita, I'm sorry about yesterday."

"But what about my turtle?"

"Let me think."

Jerry bounced as he thought. But all he could think about was the lump somewhere below his chest. He couldn't worry about a collapsed turtle.

"Are you still thinking, Jerry?"

"Yeah." What would happen to him if the lump

didn't ever go down? Would it stay soft? Would other food stick to it until it filled up his insides? Would it turn to stone? It felt like a rock.

"Have you thought of anything yet, Jerry?"

Jerry had thought of something. "Sherita, do you have any rocks?"

"No, do you?"

"Sure. That's what you can use to fix your turtle."

"Rocks?" Sherita sounded doubtful.

"No, one rock. A round one. You can put your playclay over it and it won't sag or collapse." Jerry knew he had solved Sherita's problem. Now he could go to the playground. He hadn't lost much time yet.

"But I don't have a rock."

"Do you live near a park or a playground?"

"No, not very near."

"Tomorrow's Saturday. Couldn't your mother take you to a park so you can find a rock for your science project?" Jerry asked with desperation. How was he going to get off the phone? After yesterday, he could never hang up on her again.

"Well, I guess so. I can ask her."

"That's great. You can make a great turtle. I gotta go play soccer now."

"Are you on a soccer team?"

"No, but I'm planning to be in the spring. That's why I have to practice. Your problem is taken care of now and I gotta go play soccer."

"Where do you practice?"

"At the playground."

"Which playground?"

"It's not really a playground, just an empty lot. Now I've—"

"What empty lot?" Sherita demanded.

Jerry had never known anybody who asked so many questions. If trees could talk, Sherita would probably ask them where their roots go. Why did she want to know where his playground was? But he knew better than to answer her question with a question. "It's on Vine Street."

"Where on Vine Street?"

"Between Post and General MacArthur Boulevard. Now I've got to go. The guys will all—"

"Okay, Jerry," she interrupted him. "Bye."

To his amazement, she hung up. Jerry didn't believe in questioning his good luck. He hung up, too, and rushed out of the apartment. As he ran, the peanut butter lump dropped. Then it disappeared, and Jerry felt great.

CHAPTER 8

Jerry figured he must have broken some records to get to the playground first, even after talking to Sherita.

"It's gonna be soccer today, sports fans," he yelled happily as the first of Tank's army arrived.

Jerry's team won the toss. Ricky took the ball out and kicked it straight to Jerry. The army was all around him, yelping like a pack of hounds as Jerry worked his way down the field, guarding the ball from their darting feet. All he needed was one clear kick. Their goalie was slow.

Jerry watched for an opening. He took deep

gulps of air. He felt alive all over. Even his hair felt alive. This was what he was born for . . . guarding, running, planning, being on his own with the ball, Jerry couldn't imagine anything more fun. It was the greatest feeling in the world.

Jerry lofted the ball over two fallen army players before they could scramble to their feet. Ricky picked it up and passed it to John, who passed it back to Jerry before Tank and his team could decide who had the ball. Now Jerry had his opening. He let fly with a tremendous kick.

Their goalie had planted his feet in the middle of the cage. Jerry kicked the ball to the far right. The goalie lunged, but not far or fast enough, and the ball hit the side of the building behind him with a satisfying smack that sounded better than music to Jerry's ears.

Tank's lieutenant took the ball out. He aimed it straight at Tank, but Jerry was waiting for it. He snagged the ball, dribbled it downfield, and made another goal before the army knew they'd lost the ball. The goalie lunged for it, but tripped over his shoelace. "No fair," he said.

"It is fair," Joel said as he blew his whistle. "Players are responsible for their equipment. That means shoelaces. Hurry up and get it tied."

The goalie made a big show of tying a double knot. Then he tied the other one the same way. Just as he jerked it tight, Jerry saw something out of the corner of his eye, something small with pigtails.

He turned and saw a little girl standing on the sidewalk.

This time Tank took the ball out. He passed it to his lieutenant, but Jerry darted by and snagged it again. As he dribbled downfield in a zigzag pattern, he came closer to the little girl. He thought she was about the size of a second grader. She was watching the game.

Someone zipped the ball away from Jerry. Jerry's attention snapped back to the game. He tore out in pursuit, caught up, and kicked out before the other player could defend the ball. Ricky was there to pick it up and take it to the goal.

Jerry looked back at the kid. It couldn't be, he thought. It had to be a coincidence. Sherita wouldn't have come to his playground.

"Time out," he called, and ran over to check.

"Are you Jerry?" she asked.

"Sherita?" She was wearing a red sweatshirt with a kitten on the front and green corduroys with a ladybug on one knee. Her black hair was in braids that ended in plastic kitten barrettes. She had light brown skin and lively brown eyes. She grinned at him, and he saw the hole where her front teeth were missing. "Oh, no, Sherita," he groaned. "What are you doing here?"

"I wanted to see you, Jerry."

"But how did you get here?"

"I came on the bus. It comes right down General MacArthur Boulevard. I ride it with my mother when we go to the library on Saturdays."

"Sherita, aren't you supposed to stay in your apartment after school?" Jerry asked. He knew that was her mother's rule.

"Yes." She looked down at her feet. She wore red sneakers. There was a tiny hole in the toe of the left one.

What was he going to do with her? She was too little to be running around loose in the city. "You can't stay here, Sherita. It's getting late. You'll have to go back home."

"But I just got here, Jerry. Can't I stay with you?" She looked up at him.

Jerry groaned. Why did she have to have such big brown eyes and be so little? He glanced around. It was getting late. There was no bus that went straight back up MacArthur. She would have to change at least once on the return trip. Jerry looked back at Sherita. She was still watching him, waiting for him to tell her what to do.

She was so trusting. Jerry knew what he had to do. He didn't want to but he had to. He couldn't send Sherita off on a bunch of buses by herself. She might get lost or kidnapped. She might ride the wrong bus and be halfway to Canada before she even knew it.

Why me? he thought. Why did she have to pick me? And why today? Today when he was at last playing soccer again? Jerry stood for a minute, putting off the decision to end his soccer game. "Wait here," he told her. Then he walked back to the two teams, who were watching him.

"I've got to go," he said. The words felt like rocks pelting him. "I can't finish the game. You can play basketball if you want to change games."

"Why?" asked Joel.

"I've gotta take her home," Jerry said without enthusiasm.

Tank's friends erupted with yells and whistles. "Jerry's got a girlfriend!" Tank said, snickering.

"Don't be dumb," Jerry said. He picked up his soccer ball and walked back to Sherita as the guys chanted, "Jerry's got a girlfriend."

Jerry looked at Joel and shrugged. Joel and Jerry's other friends stared. He knew they didn't know what to think. They knew he would never leave a soccer game unless both of his legs were broken or something else was really wrong.

"Come on," he said to Sherita. "I'll take you home."

At first Jerry planned to take Sherita only as far as her second bus stop. But as they walked to the first one, she slipped her hand into his. She seemed so sure that he would take care of her. It gave him a funny feeling. He knew he would have to take her all the way to her building.

He dug into his pocket as they waited at the bus stop. It was lucky he had some change, he thought. He had enough for their fares and his coming back.

"You shouldn't have come here, Sherita," Jerry said when they were on the bus.

"I wanted to see what you look like." She grinned and showed the gap where her front teeth were missing.

"I know your mother wouldn't like it."

"I won't tell her."

"What if she calls up and you aren't there?

She might call the police," Jerry said.

"I never thought about that. But she only calls once."

"She might call again."

"Aren't you glad to see me a little?"

"That has nothing to do with it," Jerry said. He was irritated that she just did what she wanted to do without thinking about what might happen. "We could both get into a lot of trouble. And you kept me from doing what I like to do more than anything in the world."

"What's that?"

"Play soccer."

"I'm sorry, Jerry."

Her eyes seemed to grow bigger. A fat tear overflowed from the corner of one. She sniffed.

Oh no, Jerry thought. Not that. "It's all right, Sherita. Don't cry. I'm glad uh . . ." he stopped. He couldn't say he was glad she came and interrupted his soccer game and made him feel responsible for her so he had to give up his game and take her home. He couldn't say he was glad that he might be late getting home, and his mother would find out that he had left the playground and gone across the city on buses, which was against all the rules on the refrigerator. But he knew he had to say something to comfort Sherita and stop her from crying.

"Um, I'm glad that we finally got to meet," he said.

"Are you really, Jerry?"

"Yes, I am," he said as she looked up at him with shining eyes. It wasn't totally untrue. He had wondered what she looked like, too, and now he knew. She looked exactly as he had thought she would. Only she was smaller and not as bossy.

Jerry wished the bus would hurry. Rush hour was starting now and traffic would be slower going home. But at last they reached her apartment building. "Go straight up to your apartment now," he told her as he turned to go back to the bus stop.

"Can I still call you up, Jerry?" she called after him.

Jerry froze. How could he say no?

"Okay, sure, Sherita. You can still call me up sometimes."

"Bye, Jerry."

"Bye." Jerry headed back down the street toward the bus stop. He didn't have to turn his head to see her. A picture of her was glued behind his eyelids. He had been face-to-face with her and hadn't told her not to call him up. In fact, he had told her to call him sometime. Plus he could be in big trouble if his mother found out he had left the playground. So why did he feel so good?

CHAPTER 9

The streets were crowded with rush hour traffic by the time Jerry got back on the bus. The sky had that murky purple look it got just before dusk, and there were deep shadows between the buildings. It would be dark before he got home.

Jerry was worried. He knew he was going to be late. If his mom got home before he did, she might think something had happened to him. She might even call the police.

The bus crept down General MacArthur Boulevard, stopping at each corner to let a few people off and more passengers on. There were people standing in the aisles holding onto straps, the backs of seats, each other; people going home from work, just like his mom. Maybe she was caught in a traffic jam, too, he thought, hoping it was so.

The bus lurched forward a few feet, then came to another standstill. Horns blared but traffic didn't move. Minutes passed as Jerry watched the daylight disappearing. He couldn't sit on this bus all night. He had to do something.

Jerry jumped up and pulled the cord to be let off. He squeezed through the passengers to the back door but the door was closed. The bus driver wouldn't open it until the next stop. It was so close. Jerry could see the red sign with the white letters spelling BUS STOP just ahead.

The bus moved an inch. Jerry let out a sigh of relief. Then the bus stopped again. It moved another inch. Then it stopped. Jerry thought if he ever got off this bus, he would never stop running.

The bus finally rolled to the stop. The door opened. Jerry burst out and hit the ground at a run. He sprinted until he reached his building. He sped up the stairs and down the hall. He slowed down as he approached his door. He put his key in the lock and turned it gently. He opened the door.

The light was on in the kitchen. He hadn't left it on. That meant his mother was home.

"Jerry, where have you been?"

She didn't sound upset, Jerry thought.

Then she came out of the kitchen. She had the telephone receiver in her hand.

That was a bad sign. "I've been to the playground," Jerry said.

His mother gave him the look that meant she knew he wasn't telling all of the truth. She hung the receiver up. "Your friends have been home from the playground for over an hour. You have some explaining to do. Where have you been?"

Jerry began to tell her about Sherita. "There's this little girl. She followed me to the playground. She's only seven, real little. You wouldn't believe how little she is. She could probably pass for four. I had to take her home. The bus got stuck in traffic. That's why I'm late."

"I see." Jerry was glad that his mother didn't look angry. She picked up the pot holder shaped like a soccer ball he'd given her for Mother's Day. She opened the oven door and looked in. Then she turned back to Jerry.

He waited, afraid of what was coming.

"You felt responsible for this little girl. I'm glad that you were, Jerry. But you should have brought her home with you. We could have called her parents and made arrangements to take her home."

"I think she only has a mother."

"We could have called her mother."

"I didn't think about that," Jerry said.

"That's the problem, Jerry. You didn't think. That's why your dad and I made these rules. You have to follow them. When you are older, you can make your own rules. By then, maybe you will have learned to think things out."

Jerry listened to his mother with a sinking heart. He knew he was going to be punished. But how?

"Until then," his mother went on, "you will have to abide by our rules. I'll discuss the details with your dad when he calls. Now give me your door key."

Jerry froze. Not his latchkey. Surely she wouldn't take away his latchkey.

His mother held out her hand. "Come on, Jerry. We told you what would happen if you disobeyed the rules."

Slowly Jerry slipped the chain over his head. He felt as though he were underwater looking up at the world. The key banged against his nose the way it always did when he took it off. He held it out to his mother.

"Is it forever?" he asked, almost choking on the words.

"I'll discuss it with your father. Go and wash up now for supper."

Jerry wasn't hungry. He didn't think he would ever be hungry again. And if he had been hungry, he wouldn't have wanted tuna loaf with broccoli in it. Yucko. He pushed the green mess around on his plate. Why were so many bad things green? Jerry had nothing against the color. It was nice for grass and leaves and leprechauns. But not for food. Except for gumdrops and lollipops and M & M's.

In the middle of supper the phone rang. Jerry jumped, but it was somebody from his mother's office inviting her to a bridal shower. They talked for so long that Jerry was able to scrape and rinse his plate without his mother noticing that he had eaten less than three bites.

He mumbled something about studying and went to his room. He closed the door behind him.

He wanted to get away from the smell of the tuna loaf, he told himself. But he also wanted to hide from the world.

Jerry sat on the edge of his bed. His arms hung down, dangling between his knees. He stared at his wall of posters and clippings, a jumble of colors and newsprint. What was he going to do now?

He had tried to do the right thing about Sherita. It had seemed right at the time. If only the buses hadn't been so slow.

If only Sherita had dialed one different digit, she would have gotten somebody else on the phone.

If only he had hung up on her the first time she called.

If only . . .

But Jerry knew there was nothing to be gained by if onlys. He had taken Sherita home, but in doing it he had gotten himself in the worst trouble he'd ever been in. Now all he could do was wait for his dad to call.

It seemed to Jerry that the phone had never rung so much. It rang more that night than it usually did in a week.

The first call after supper was Joel.

"What happened, Jerry? Who was that little girl?"

Jerry explained. "She's just a kid I know, the one who has been calling me. I had to take her home and then the bus was late. I'm in big trouble."

"Yeah, I know. Your mom called my mom looking for you. What are they going to do to you?"

"She took my latchkey," Jerry whispered the words. He couldn't say them out loud.

"For how long?"

"I don't know yet. She's got to talk to Dad. He's supposed to call tonight. I better get off the phone."

"Okay."

When the phone rang again, Jerry thought it might be one of his gang. But it was one of Tank's lieutenants. He sniggered, "Jerry's got a girlfriend," then hung up before Jerry could tell which one it was. Jerry felt like bashing the telephone into every one of those guys.

The next call was the one he'd been dreading, his father calling from Omaha. Jerry waited in the living room. His mother had taken his latchkey away, maybe forever. He waited to hear what else his parents would do to him.

After what seemed like three years, his mother came in and sat down. "That was Dad. He was in a rush and only had a few minutes to talk. He agrees with me that you used poor judgment. You have to understand that the rules are not to be broken."

"I didn't mean to break the rules," Jerry protested. "I just didn't know what else to do."

"We know that, Jerry. But you did break them. So we have decided that for one week you will go to a sitter."

It was worse than Jerry had thought. "Who?"

"Mr. Burt Feeney."

"Who is he?"

"You've met him. He used to work at Dad's company."

"I don't remember him. Was he a driver?"

"No, he was a checker. He's retired now. Dad has given him rides to his daughter's house for visits from time to time. He says he will be glad for your company this week. Actually, it is working out quite well. He only lives three blocks from here, closer to the school than we do."

It wasn't working out well for Jerry. He hardly dared to ask. "Can I still go to the playground then?"

"No, Jerry. You must go straight to Mr. Feeney's house and stay there. After a week of punishment, maybe you will remember that the rules are to be obeyed. This is really important, Jerry. Do you understand?"

Jerry nodded. He understood. He had no hope now. He had been sentenced to a week without soccer. A whole week. Maybe the last week before winter. Now he would never be a soccer star.

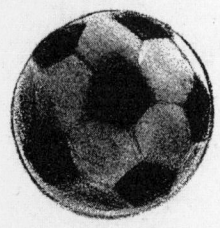

CHAPTER 10

Monday morning was a clear, crisply cold day, a perfect day for soccer. Jerry felt only half dressed without his latchkey under his shirt. He couldn't let anybody know he wasn't a latchkey kid anymore. It was too humiliating. He imagined the army's jeers as he tied his sneakers. "Mama's baby" was probably the nicest of them.

They wouldn't find out. Not if he could help it. Jerry rummaged in his top drawer until he found an old key. He slipped it onto a shoelace, knotted the ends around his neck, and dropped the key under his shirt. He looked in the mirror. It was smaller than his real latchkey, but hopefully nobody would notice the difference. If anybody did, Jerry planned to say that his lock had been changed.

But he, Jerry, would know. The old key didn't feel like his latchkey. It felt like a stone hung around his neck.

Then there was the problem of the playground. How was he going to explain his absence to the army?

"Tell them I've gone to the dentist," Jerry told Joel at school.

"All week?"

"I guess so."

"But nobody goes every day for a week," Joel objected.

"Well, make up something. Tell them my grandmother is here or something."

Joel looked doubtful. "I'll try."

After school Jerry went to the address his mother had given him. He walked slowly along the sidewalk. He was in no hurry to get there. His mother had said he had met Mr. Feeney, but Jerry didn't remember him. It must have been while he was still a baby.

Jerry kicked a Coke can for a while. But it was

no fun unless he could run and lift the can and race with it as it spun high overhead. What was the use of doing that if his soccer career was already over? When the can rolled into the gutter, Jerry left it there.

The apartment building looked a lot like Jerry's. Mr. Feeney lived on the third floor. Jerry climbed the stairs and went down a dark hall until he found number six. There was a brass card holder on the door. A card in it said B. F. FEENEY. Jerry knocked.

"No need to bang. I can still hear as well as you can," said the man who opened the door on Jerry's third knock.

He was a thin old man with sparse gray hair. He wore gray wool pants and a gray cardigan sweater over a gray and blue plaid shirt. On his nose were thick-lensed glasses with black rims. "Come in, boy. Don't let the heat out."

Jerry went in. The apartment smelled like medicine. It was dark. All the blinds on the windows were closed. Jerry tripped over something that felt like a footstool, but it could have been a giant mushroom.

"Watch where you're going, boy," Mr. Feeney said.

The living room was lit by a large TV screen. "Marsha, you must listen to me," an actor was saying. "Phillip, darling, it's for the best," an actress replied.

Mr. Feeney went back to his chair, an over-stuffed armchair with a fat ottoman in front of it for his feet.

"Mr. Feeney," Jerry began.

"Ssshhh, I want to hear this," Mr. Feeney interrupted.

Jerry had meant to ask him where he should do his homework. As his eyes adjusted to the dark, he saw that this was a one-room apartment, a studio apartment. There was nowhere else to go but the bathroom. Jerry sat down on the edge of a hard sofa. What was he supposed to do now?"

When the commercial came on, Mr. Feeney turned to Jerry. "Now then, I suppose you'd like a snack?"

This was better. "Yes sir, I would."

"Good." Mr. Feeney went to the kitchen alcove. Jerry noticed that his feet were in bedroom boots, the kind that are lined with fake furry stuff.

Mr. Feeney made noises in the kitchen. He came back in a few seconds with a saucer. On it were two halves of an apple. He took one and offered the other to Jerry. "Boy needs a snack after school," he said almost to himself. "I know I always did."

Jerry ate his apple half right away. He was always hungry after school. Mr. Feeney nibbled his half for the rest of the afternoon, in between doses of cough syrup, lozenges, and nasal spray. His medicines were crowded on a small table at his elbow. Jerry thought he must have half a drugstore there.

The telephone was on the table, too. When it rang, Mr. Feeney answered with a loud, "Hello? Who? Yes, he's here. You want to speak to him?"

He handed the receiver to Jerry. "It's your mother."

"Hi, Mom," Jerry said without enthusiasm.

"Hello, Jerry. I'm just checking to see that you got there safely. Everything all right?"

"Sure, Mom. Just great."

"It's not forever, Jerry."

"I know." Jerry said good-bye and hung up. It was forever to him.

The TV program came to an end. Jerry hoped something good would come on now. Maybe a sports program.

After a string of commercials, organ music

oozed from the TV. An announcer said, "Hospital Hearts," as the screen showed a hand putting a stethoscope on lacy valentine hearts. Jerry couldn't believe anybody would watch this.

He wished he could talk to somebody, anybody. He even wished he could talk to Sherita. Maybe he could call her. He could tell her how she'd got him into trouble.

"May I use your telephone, Mr. Feeney?" he asked during a commercial.

"Is it an emergency?"

"No, I guess not."

"Then the answer is no. I have basic budget service and pay for every call."

Jerry sank back on the sofa. He would have to wait it out. His friends were all out on the playground. He was stuck here in soap opera land with the stingiest man in the world. Jerry had never heard of giving somebody half of an apple. He could see a banana sticking up in a fruit bowl on the counter in the kitchen. Jerry's mouth watered for that banana.

There was nothing to do but watch TV. Jerry's attention was drawn into "Hospital Hearts" against his will. He found himself watching Dr. Valentine Monroe, who was being sued for malpractice by Arlene Alewine because she had a tiny scar on her throat after nearly choking on a canapé of caviar. Jerry didn't know what a canapé of caviar was but he planned never to eat one. Dr. Monroe saved Arlene but Arlene was suing anyway because her lawyer Michael was in love with Dr. Monroe. Arlene wanted him to be in love with her. Michael's ex-wife Carlotta was in love with Dr. Joel Mansfield who wanted to marry Dr. Monroe. Dr. Mansfield used to be married to Arlene, too. Later he was married to Melissa Talbot, a therapist, but now she was married to Dr. James Turner. There was something mysterious about Dr. Turner but nobody knew what it was except that it had happened in medical school.

Jerry figured it out. Dr. Turner had probably secretly been married to Dr. Monroe and had never gotten divorced. That's why he acted so strangely.

"Hospital Hearts" ended with Dr. Turner hiding in a closet while Dr. Monroe walked by with Michael.

Next came "The Sands of Time." It opened with a sand dune blowing around in the wind while waves lashed it furiously. Dorothea was in love with Archer Breckinridge, whose ex-wife

Avis vowed she was going to get him back or else. Archer's secretary Iris was spying on him for Avis because she was in love with Avis's brother Tony who was blackmailing his sister because she once did something terrible.

Jerry thought the terrible thing she did was wear two-foot-long fake eyelashes and blink them all the time. She was driving him crazy with her whiny voice and batting eyelashes.

Jerry was glassy eyed when his mother called for him to come home. How was he going to stand a week of this?

The next day Jerry packed a survival kit. He put in a snack, which he ate on the way to Mr. Feeney's. He also put in a flashlight to do his homework by, but Mr. Feeney said it bothered his eyes. So every day Jerry had to listen to the problems of the soap opera people.

Mr. Feeney had told Jerry's mother that he would be glad of Jerry's company. But Jerry thought the soap opera people were all the company Mr. Feeney needed. He didn't talk to Jerry. He talked to the soap opera people. He would nod when one of them said something he agreed with or he would say things like, "That's telling her," or "Don't go in there," or "Don't listen to him, Dr. Monroe," or "Watch out for Archer."

Mr. Feeney had a subscription to a magazine called *TV Chronicles.* It told all about the actors playing the parts and summarized all the episodes in case you had to go to the dentist and missed an episode.

"You wouldn't believe this guy," Jerry exploded to Joel on the phone that night. "All he ever does besides watch these shows on TV is suck on cough drops. Today he told me he was seriously getting a sore throat. He wore two mufflers around his neck. He looked like a skinny turtle!"

"My grandmother is like that. She wears a muffler around her nose sometimes. She watches the soap operas, too. Once my uncle was sick while he was staying with her. He got hooked and when he went home, he started taping them on his VCR while he was at work so he could watch them when he got home."

"Yuck. Grown-ups are weird. I don't know why they don't like cartoons."

"Yeah," Joel agreed.

"How am I going to get through a whole week?" Jerry moaned.

———

It was the longest week of Jerry's life. And when it ended, Dr. Monroe was locked in the X-ray room, Iris was locked in a closet in Archer's hunting lodge, Dorothea was locked in a tiger cage with the tiger in it, and Dr. Turner had fallen over a waterfall.

As Jerry was putting on his jacket Mr. Feeney said, "To celebrate the end of your week with me, I bought a special treat for you." He held out a small white paper bag to Jerry.

"Thanks, Mr. Feeney." Jerry looked inside. At first he thought Mr. Feeney had given him a bag of goldfish. Then he saw that the goldfish were four pieces of that awful orange slice candy, the kind that is sugary on the outside and horribly slimy on the inside.

Mr. Feeney watched with an expectant look. Jerry took out a slice of the candy. He bit through the gritty sweet coating, then swallowed the bite whole without chewing.

"Have one, Mr. Feeney." He offered the bag.

"No, boy. These are all for you," Mr. Feeney said. He was smiling. Jerry had never seen him smile before.

"They're awfully good," Jerry said. He took another bite.

"That was my favorite candy when I was a boy," Mr. Feeney said. "We used to ride into town every Saturday in the wagon behind our old mule, Red. Momma would give us a nickel for candy for all of us. These orange slices were the most you could get for a nickel. We each got half a slice."

The orange bite stuck in Jerry's throat. He didn't know what to say. He couldn't imagine Mr. Feeney as a little boy riding all the way to town and only getting half of an orange slice.

He swallowed hard. "Well, thanks again, Mr. Feeney. This is real good candy. I'll just save the rest for after supper. Mom doesn't like for me to eat this close to supper."

"Quite right. I don't know what I was thinking of." Mr. Feeney smiled at Jerry. The wrinkles on his cheeks rode up to his eyes and made him look even more like a turtle. "I enjoyed your company this week, Jerry." But as Jerry was going out the door Mr. Feeney said, "I can't wait until next week to find out what happened to all my friends. If you want to know, you can give a call."

Jerry said good-bye. He didn't tell Mr. Feeney that he hoped he, Jerry, never found out what happened.

CHAPTER 11

Jerry ran on air all the way home from Mr. Feeney's.

"Faster than the speed of light, sports fans!" gasped the announcer.

Jerry raced up the stairs to his floor. The wonderful smell of hamburgers reached him as soon as he stepped into the hall. He followed the trail of hamburger smell all the way to his door. His mother never cooked hamburgers. It meant his dad was home.

The door wasn't locked. Jerry flung it open. "Dad!" he yelled happily.

His father was in the kitchen. He was a tall man with dark hair and brown eyes like Jerry's. He wore a blue denim apron over his jeans and plaid shirt, the sleeves rolled to the elbows. On the apron in big red letters it said: MAN IN THE KITCHEN. Jerry grabbed him around the waist in a bear hug.

"Hold on there, sport," his father said, laughing. "Let me flip this burger."

He turned the burger over with an oversized spatula and then grabbed Jerry and hugged him back.

"Jeeps, Dad, this has been an awful week." Jerry told him about Mr. Feeney, but his dad didn't seem to think it was so awful. He laughed.

"What an experience, Jerry. Bert was always worried about his health. I remember him sucking those awful-smelling cough drops when he went with me on cross-country hauls. It was like having a hospital in the cab with me."

"He has a whole drugstore on the table by his chair," Jerry said. "All week he only gave me half of an apple for a snack. Then when I was leaving today he gave me this bag of orange candy. Next to licorice, it's the worst candy in the world. He says it's his favorite."

Jerry's dad laughed. "I should go to see Bert. He and Dotty fed me a lot of meals before I married your mother. Trouble is, I'm home so little that I like to spend my time with my family. Maybe you and I can go to see him one day, Jerry."

Jerry hoped it wouldn't be too soon. Mr. Feeney would probably want to catch him up on everything that had happened on the soap operas. "Not this weekend. I need to play soccer. I didn't get to play all week. My muscles are all soft from sitting on Mr. Feeney's sofa. I need a workout."

"I guess you do. That reminds me, I have something that belongs to you."

His father opened a drawer in the kitchen and took out a key, Jerry's key. "You'll be needing this."

Jerry took the key but he didn't put it on. He didn't want his father to see the other key around his neck. He put the latchkey in his pocket and kept his hand on it for a long time, curling his fingers around the key, feeling its shape pressed against his palm. He never wanted to lose his latchkey again.

"Next time," his father said, "think before you break the rules. Now how about some supper?"

Jerry gave him another hug. He was glad his dad wasn't going to give him a lecture. "Jeeps, I'm glad you're home, Dad. Mom has been feeding me tuna fish every night almost."

His dad ruffled Jerry's hair. "Nothing wrong with tuna. It's good for the brain. It should improve your schoolwork a lot."

"Yeah, Dad," Jerry said. "But not my taste buds. I've been hungry for a hamburger."

"Soccer players need red meat, huh?"

"They sure do. I wish you'd tell that to Mom."

"She thinks fish is just as good for you," his dad said as he turned the burgers again.

"She'll be sorry when I start growing fins," Jerry said. "When can we eat?"

"Soon as your mother gets home." His father checked his watch. "Which should be any minute now. How about setting the table?"

"Okay." Jerry went to wash his hands. His heart felt as light as his feet. It was going to be a great weekend.

On Saturday, Jerry and his dad kicked the ball around the playground. And on Sunday, they went to a soccer game at City College. Jerry jumped as he watched the players. His knees twitched and his toes itched to be out there running and kicking the ball, too. There was nothing in the world as great as playing soccer. Except being with his dad at a soccer game.

Jerry's latchkey bumped agreeably beneath his shirt as he ran to school on Monday. It felt much better than the substitute key. He pulled his key out before class started and checked the clasp on the chain. He knew the clasp was okay but he wanted people to see his key. Joel gave him a thumbs-up sign from across the room.

Jerry hadn't talked to Sherita since the day he had taken her home. He had almost forgotten about her during his week with Mr. Feeney. His problems had taken all his attention. He was surprised when she called after school. Surely she would have given up after a week with nobody answering the phone at his house. Anybody else would. But not Sherita. She never gave up. Jerry knew he should have called her and told her what had happened and why he hadn't been home. But he had been so miserable.

"Hi, Jerry. This is Sherita. Where have you been?"

"I had to go to a sitter all last week. I was being punished for taking you home. I didn't get to play soccer all week." And it was all your fault, his tone implied.

"I'm sorry, Jerry. Honest."

"Why'd you do it?"

"I just wanted to meet you. I didn't mean to get you in trouble." She sounded like she was going to cry.

"That's okay, Sherita. Just don't do it again."

"I won't," she sniffled. "Thank you for taking me home."

"I said it's okay, Sherita. Uh, how's your turtle project?"

"That's why I called. I need to know some things about turtles. Where do they sleep?"

Didn't she know anything? "In their shells," Jerry replied, biting off the "stupid" he wanted to add.

"But where are their shells when they are sleeping? In the water? Or do they burrow in mud? Or what?"

"Jeeps, I don't know. Get a book and find out." Sherita asked more questions than anybody he'd ever met. He bet she stayed awake all night thinking them up. But he had to admit she never gave up. And he never knew what she was going to ask him next.

"Can't you look in your 'cyclopedia for me?"

"No, I can't," Jerry told her. "I need to play soccer. I didn't get to play all last week. I have to go now."

But not before he checked the encyclopedia for the sleeping habits of turtles.

It seemed that nothing had changed with Sherita. She was as determined as ever to keep Jerry on the phone and make him miss soccer. She seemed to think he knew the answers to everything and if he didn't, he would find out for her. She depended on him to help her. Jerry had to help her. He couldn't let her down.

Jerry didn't have a brother or sister, but now he thought he knew what it was like to be a big brother. Sherita had sort of adopted him to be hers.

He decided to ask her a question. "Sherita, why do you call me up every day and ask me all these questions?"

" 'Cause I need help on my project."

Jerry had a feeling that there was something more behind it. "You can ask the school librarian to help you," he said.

Sherita didn't say anything.

"I mean, maybe the librarian couldn't tell you

90

how to make a playclay turtle, but she could help you find a book about turtles that would have all the answers in it."

Still Sherita didn't reply.

"You're not being fair, Sherita. I've answered your questions. Now you have to answer mine. Why do you call me up every day at the same time?"

" 'Cause I'm scared."

Scared? What could she be scared of? "You weren't scared to take the bus all by yourself to the playground."

"That's different. There were people around. Aren't you scared?"

"No. Why should I be?"

"Is anybody home when you get there?"

"No. Nobody's here."

"Nobody's here when I come home and it's scary," she whispered.

"Why is it scary?" Jerry asked. "Why are you whispering?"

"It's so quiet. And empty. And something might be there," she finished in a rush.

"What do you mean, something might be there?" Jerry was puzzled. What was the matter with Sherita?

"You know, bears or burglars or something."

So that was it. "Aw, Sherita, you're imagining things. There's nothing to be afraid of. If your apartment is empty, that means nobody is there and you're safe," Jerry told her with what he thought was perfect logic.

"I didn't say somebody might be there. I said some*thing,*" Sherita corrected him, "or bears or burglars. That's not somebody."

"Same thing," Jerry said. "It's all your imagination. Why don't you turn on the TV? Then there will be voices and you won't feel alone." He thought of Mr. Feeney.

"Our TV's broke. It's at the shop getting fixed but it's taking a long time."

"How about a radio then?" he suggested.

"I don't have one."

She didn't have a tape player either. She didn't even have a wind-up musical toy. Jerry ran out of suggestions. He was also running out of time, he thought, as he noticed the kitchen clock. Jerry didn't quite know why but he felt that it was his responsibility to solve Sherita's problem about being scared. Of all the telephone numbers in the city, she had picked his. It was almost as though she had especially chosen him to protect her from the monsters of her imagination. But he didn't know how. Just talking on the phone every day wasn't really the answer. He couldn't talk to her every day until her mother came home. That wasn't it. And besides, he had his own things to do.

"I guess I gotta go now, Sherita. My friends are waiting for me," he said at last.

"Do you have to?"

"Yeah. If I don't practice every chance I get, I might not get on a soccer team in the spring. I can't practice in the winter and it's getting colder every day." Jerry hoped she would understand. You had to practice to be a soccer star.

"Well, okay, Jerry, if you have to," Sherita said, but she didn't sound happy about it.

Jerry wasn't either but he didn't know what to do. He hung the phone up slowly. He didn't even run to the playground.

CHAPTER 12

Two weeks. Jerry wrote the two words in the margin of his science notebook. He hadn't been first at the playground in two weeks. He hadn't played soccer in two weeks except on the weekend and that wasn't enough. He had to solve Sherita's problem so he could get to the playground first.

He wondered if she had been scared of bears before she became a latchkey kid. He could tell her that there was nothing to be scared of, but he knew it wouldn't do any good. He remembered when he was in the second grade and his mother took him to swim classes at the Y. He had been afraid of the deep water. He had imagined there were monsters at the bottom. His mother and the instructor had told him not to be afraid, but it hadn't helped. Not until he had learned to swim and could skim over the top of the deep part had he gotten over his fear.

Once you do something like that, you aren't afraid anymore. But Sherita went home every day to the empty apartment, and still she was scared enough to call him up every day. Jerry had a feeling that Sherita was more lonesome than afraid. If she were really afraid, just talking to him on the phone wouldn't be enough to dispel her fear. He couldn't blame her for wanting someone to talk to. But all the same he couldn't be her company every day. He had to practice soccer.

His spelling book was open in front of him but he didn't see the page with the day's lesson on it. Instead, Jerry saw himself standing with one foot on a bear he had slain with a bow and arrow, a giant bear with long sharp teeth. Sherita was wearing a pink princess dress with a little gold crown over her braids. She would take his sword and touch him on each shoulder and the top of his head. "Arise, Sir Jerry," she would say.

There was a poke in his ribs. Jerry was annoyed.

Didn't Sherita know you didn't dub a knight in the ribs?

"Pssst, Jerry." It was Joel. He was poking Jerry with a pencil. "Get out your math book. Page sixty-six."

Jerry slid his book out of his desk. What had happened to spelling? He'd find out from Joel later. He was glad Mrs. Brent hadn't noticed his daydreaming. He tried to concentrate on his work for the rest of the afternoon.

Jerry was the third kid out of the school after the bell rang. He found a can to kick and started down his alley route.

The can skimmed along the alley, hardly touching the ground. Jerry burrowed down into his jacket as the wind whipped around a corner. Soon there would be snow on the ground. Jerry gave the can a sharp kick. It spurted forward.

"Another missile, soccer fans, an incredible kick by the one and only JJ," the announcer yelled over the roar of the crowd.

Spurred by the cheers, Jerry picked up speed and passed two boys throwing rocks. As Jerry whizzed by, he saw a small gray animal crouched in a doorway. A cornered rat, he thought. But he noticed it had a furry tail. Rats' tails, he knew, were stringy.

Jerry slowed down and stopped. He didn't want to go back. But the boys were throwing rocks at a kitten, a kitten that was smaller than a rat.

Jerry turned and went back. The boys were intent on their rock throwing and didn't pay any attention to him.

"Bull's-eye!" the taller one shouted.

The kitten yelped and spat as it tried to climb the door frame. But the metal frame was too slick for the kitten's claws and it slid down into a small heap of fur.

Jerry studied the boys. One was bigger than he was but the other was much smaller. He had never seen either of them before. He picked up his can and walked past them down the alley where he had just come. He set the can down on its end and made his plan.

First he took off his backpack and held it as he backed away. Then he ran towards the can and gave it a tremendous kick, a goal kick. Like a bullet the can streaked past the two boys and hit the brick wall in front of them. It bounced off the wall and hit the big boy smack in the chest.

Bull's-eye!

While the boys' attention was on the can, Jerry raced between them, scooped up the kitten, and stuck it into his backpack. Then he ran like the wind, like JJ, the world-famous soccer player.

Jerry could hear the two boys yelling at him as they realized what had happened and chased after him. But he wasn't worried. Nobody in the whole fourth grade and most of the fifth could catch him.

Jerry held the backpack against his chest and sprinted down the alley. The kitten didn't struggle. He hoped it had enough air.

The sounds of the two boys behind him grew fainter, then stopped. They had given up the chase. Jerry was glad because he had to wait for three cars to pass before he could cross the street.

In the apartment, he put the backpack on the kitchen floor and waited for the kitten to crawl out. But nothing in the backpack moved. Had the kitten suffocated? Jerry nudged the backpack with his foot. Still no movement. He picked up the end of the canvas and shook it gently. The kitten tumbled out onto the floor and looked around, blinking with surprise. It didn't seem to be afraid.

Jerry touched its head with one finger. It felt

soft. He stroked it. "You're a cute little guy," he told the kitten.

At the sound of his voice, the kitten looked up until it fell over backward. Jerry laughed. The kitten mewed.

"I'll bet you're hungry," Jerry said.

The kitten mewed again.

Jerry took a carton of milk out of the refrigerator and poured some in a bowl. But the milk felt awfully cold to him. Maybe he should warm it some like they do for babies. He poured about half a cup into a saucepan and put it on the stove to warm the way his dad had showed him. The kitten tried to follow him around the kitchen. It was the skinniest kitten Jerry had ever seen. Its bones stuck out in angles all over and its back sort of caved in on itself. He added some sugar to the milk.

How did you fatten up a kitten in a hurry? His mother always told him to eat his eggs because they would make him grow. Maybe the same thing was good for kittens. Jerry broke an egg in a bowl and beat it a little with a fork. Then he added the warm, sugared milk. He stuck his finger in and tasted it. Not bad. For a raw egg.

He put the bowl down in front of the kitten but

all it did was sit there and look at him. Jerry stuck his finger in the milk again and put it to the kitten's mouth. The kitten smelled his finger, then licked it. Jerry led it with his finger until its mouth was in the milk. The kitten began to lap the milk with tiny sounds as regular as the ticking of a watch.

The phone rang. Jerry talked to his mother as he watched the kitten. He didn't tell her about it. He knew their apartment building had a rule against pets. He didn't know what he was going to do, but one thing was certain: He wasn't going to put it back on the street to starve and be hurt by mean kids.

"Don't go to the playground today, Jerry," his mother said before she hung up. "I think it's going to rain. There have already been some sprinkles here."

"Aw, Mom," Jerry protested. But he did it half-heartedly because he didn't want to leave the kitten.

Jerry didn't tell Sherita about the kitten when she called, either. He listened to her talk about her project and even looked up turtle care in captivity for her without her asking.

But as soon as the kitten finished drinking its

egg-milk and began washing its paws, he hung up.

"I got to go now, Sherita," Jerry told her. "I've got some things to do."

"Are you going to the playground?"

"No, I have some things to do here."

"Okay, Jerry. Bye."

Jerry picked up the kitten. It hardly weighed anything and it was dirty. He couldn't even tell what color it was. It probably had fleas, too. The thought made him itch.

"Little guy, you've got to have a bath."

Jerry ran warm water in the bathroom sink. He added some of his mother's bubble stuff. The kitten didn't seem to mind the water or the bubbles. It batted the bubbles with its paws and looked surprised when they popped. It purred contentedly as he scrubbed its matted fur, which was still gray under all the dirt. Then he rinsed it again and again until the rinse water was clear. He dried the kitten carefully with a towel. Then he dried it more with his mother's hair dryer set on low. The kitten yawned and Jerry could see its sharp little teeth like tiny needles in its pink mouth.

Jerry tried to think what else a kitten needed. A bed. That was easy. A soft, old shirt wadded up made a good one. And a cat box. Jerry remembered his grandmother's cat Marlowe used a box filled with kitty litter for its bathroom. He didn't have any kitty litter. Instead, he tore newspaper into confetti and put it in the box that had held comic books in the bottom of his closet.

As if that was what it had been waiting for, the kitten promptly jumped in the box and used it.

At least he didn't have to teach it how to do that, Jerry thought with relief. He made a ball of wadded up paper and played with the kitten until just before his mother came home.

When he heard her key in the lock, Jerry put the kitten in his closet with the box, its bed, a bowl of water, and some more egg-milk. His mother wouldn't find it before Saturday. The kitten was safe for now. But what was he going to do with the kitten when she found it?

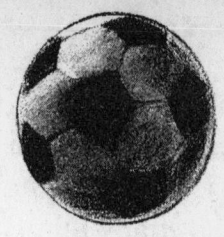

CHAPTER 13

Everything would have been just fine, Jerry thought later, if his Aunt Louise hadn't called. She wanted to know if Jerry still had his sheep costume from the third-grade play. His cousin Billy had to be a sheep in his Sunday school Christmas pageant. When Jerry got out of the shower, his mother called him into the living room. She was holding the kitten.

"Look what I found, Jerry. I went in your closet to find a sheep suit and I found a kitten suit with the kitten still in it." She laughed at her joke.

Jerry didn't see anything to laugh about. He

waited to find out what his mother was going to do. She was stroking the kitten's ears and it was purring like a motorboat. Finally he couldn't stand it any longer. "Can I keep it?"

"It's a she. I'm sorry, Jerry. She's a nice cat and you know how much I like cats. But we can't have pets in our building."

"Why not? Nobody would know."

"Mr. Jones would find out sooner or later."

"How? How would he find out? Nobody would know but us."

She shook her head. "Sometimes the super has to come in when we aren't home. To fix the plumbing or something. It's too hard to find an apartment to get ourselves evicted over a cat. I'm sorry, Jerry, but the kitten will have to go. When we have our house we can have a cat."

"That won't help this kitten. Maybe I can find her another home."

"You can try. She can stay here until Saturday, but then you will have to take her to the animal shelter."

Jerry knew what that meant. Nobody would adopt a scrawny little kitten. The city had too many apartment buildings with no-pet rules. The animal shelter would put her to sleep. He couldn't let that happen. "I'll find her a home first," he told his mother.

"I hope you can. She's a nice kitten. I'll ask at my office but I don't think it will do any good. One of the secretaries was trying to give away a whole litter of kittens a few weeks ago."

Jerry called all his friends. He was hoping they might know somebody who would take in a kitten.

"She's a good mouser," he told Ricky, who had a grandmother in the suburbs.

"I'll ask her," he promised. "But she already has three cats."

Joel called around, but everybody he knew lived in no-pet buildings, too. David's mother promised to ask at her office. John and Abe weren't home, but they probably couldn't help, either. Jerry stared at the telephone. What could he do? He hated the thought of taking the kitten to the shelter. The world was too full of kittens. Nobody would want an orphaned gray kitten as skinny as this one.

Jerry turned on the TV. There must be somebody in the world who would want a cute little kitten. He flipped through the channels. A cooking program. "Just pour it in and watch the bubbles form. Look at those nice bubbles. . . ." Jerry turned the dial. "But Ronald, Millicent knows about us . . ."

That sounds like one of Mr. Feeney's programs, Jerry thought.

Then Jerry had an inspiration. Mr. Feeney! He lived all alone. The kitten would be great company for him!

Jerry got out the phone book and looked up Feeney. He found a B. F. Feeney at the right address. Jerry dialed the number.

"Hello," Mr. Feeney answered.

"Hi, Mr. Feeney. This is Jerry Johnson. Um, how are you?" Jerry asked. Now that he was actually talking to Mr. Feeney, Jerry found it hard to just say "Do you want a cat?"

"I still have a tickle in my throat," Mr. Feeney said.

Jerry thought his voice sounded sort of croaky. "Are you taking your medicine?"

"Five times a day," Mr. Feeney said.

"Um, that's too bad, I mean that's good. Mr. Feeney, would you like a cat?" Jerry blurted, "I mean a kitten?"

"A kitten? I sure would. We always had cats on the farm. Dotty and I had cats after we were married. But after she died I moved to this building.

No pets are allowed here," Mr. Feeney said, "except fish and birds. I had to give my cat away."

"Who did you give it to?" Jerry asked hopefully.

"I gave Minnie to a friend."

"Do you think your friend would like another cat?" Jerry explained about the kitten.

"I'm sorry, boy. They moved to California a year or two ago." Mr. Feeney was silent for a few moments. Then he said, "Reckon it was more nearly five years ago. Time gets away from me."

"Well, thanks anyway, Mr. Feeney," Jerry said.

At school the next day Jerry asked everybody he knew, including teachers. The answer was the same. The people who could have pets already had them. "You'd think I could find somebody who had just lost a pet," Jerry told Joel.

When Sherita called that afternoon, he didn't even try to get off the phone. He wasn't going to the playground. He needed the afternoon to find a home for the kitten. He was running out of time. Tomorrow he would have to take the kitten to the shelter.

He felt something soft touch his ankle. He looked down. The kitten was rolling around at his feet, playing with the strap on his shoe. She didn't seem worried. She didn't know what was in store for her.

"Don't you think so?" Sherita asked.

"Huh?"

"Jerry, you aren't paying attention," Sherita scolded him.

"Um, I'm sorry Sherita. I was thinking."

"What? What were you thinking, Jerry?"

Suddenly Jerry remembered something. Something Sherita had told him a long time ago in her first phone call when she told him she was afraid of bears. She liked cats. She had told him that she liked cats. Jerry brightened. It was worth a try.

"Say, Sherita, do you know anybody who has a pet?"

"You mean like a dog?"

"Yeah. Or a cat."

"I know two people with dogs. Mrs. Falzoni lives on the floor above us. She has a poodle named Muffet. Little Miss Muffet is her real name. She's white and wears little red bows in her hair. Mrs. Falzoni lets me pet her when I see them in the elevator. And Mr. Cole has a Doberman named King. People are afraid of King because he's a Doberman but Mr. Cole says he's a pussycat."

Jerry felt his excitement growing as Sherita talked. He couldn't believe his luck. Sherita lived in an apartment building that allowed pets.

"But I don't think I know anybody with a cat. Cats probably don't have to be walked like dogs. So I never see them. Why do you want to know?"

"Oh, I was just wondering." Jerry switched the conversation to turtles.

"I have to go now," he said finally. "Um, could I come over Saturday and see you, Sherita? I could see your turtle, too."

"You want to come here? To see me?" Her voice went up and ended in a little squeal.

"Um, well, I thought I would. Since it's Saturday."

"I'll have to ask my mother. I'll call you back tonight."

Jerry didn't think he could wait that long.

Sherita called back after supper.

"My mom said you can come, Jerry. What time?"

They decided on ten o'clock. "See you tomorrow, Sherita," Jerry said.

"I think I've found you a home," he told the

kitten as he hung up. The kitten mewed and tried to climb his pants leg. Jerry scooped it up and put it on his bed. The kitten curled up and went to sleep. She wasn't worried about her future, Jerry thought. She trusted Jerry to take care of her.

Jerry went to sleep with the kitten snuggled under the covers with him. He dreamed that he was playing soccer. Tank's team were sheep, Jerry's were cats. Sherita was a cheerleader but instead of a pom-pom, she carried the kitten. As he dribbled downfield, the soccer ball turned into a can. Sherita ran into the goal with the kitten and said, "I scored, Jerry. Look, I scored, too!"

CHAPTER 14

The bus doors closed with a *whoosh*. Jerry hugged the shoe box against him. He hoped the kitten would be all right in it. He had put his old shirt in for her to lie on and punched air holes in one side. The kitten mewed softly.

"Ssshhh, kitty," he whispered. He glanced around, but nobody seemed to notice. He didn't know if pets were allowed on a bus. His mother had said it was all right as long as the kitten was in a box. "Don't stay too long," she'd said when he left. "Be home by four. Dad said he'd try to call then."

Sherita opened the door before he had time to ring the bell. "I knew it was you," she said. "I heard the elevator bell and I knew it was you."

Today she had ladybug barrettes on her braids. Her green T-shirt had horses galloping across the middle. A tall woman in jeans and a yellow sweater stood behind her.

"Mama, this is Jerry. Jerry, this is my mama, Mrs. Thomas."

"Hello, Jerry." She smiled at him. "Sherita tells me that you help her with her schoolwork sometimes. That's so nice of you."

"Yes, ma'am, Mrs. Thomas. I helped her with her turtle project."

"Do you want to see my turtle, Jerry?" Sherita asked.

"Um, sure."

She held out a lumpy playclay turtle. Jerry could see that art was not Sherita's thing. "That's a . . . uh . . . great turtle, Sherita," he said.

"What's in the box?" Sherita poked at the box Jerry held under his arm. "It has air holes in it. Is it alive, Jerry? Is it a real turtle?"

"That's a good guess. But, no, it's not a turtle." He didn't know how to tell Sherita and her mother about the kitten.

But he didn't have to. Sherita poked at the box again and the top fell off. The kitten blinked sleepily at them.

"Oh, a little kitten!" Sherita squealed.

Mrs. Thomas didn't say anything. Jerry stole a quick look at her. She didn't look mad or anything. She looked interested.

Jerry hoped the kitten would yawn. It was so cute when it did that. The kitten looked at him and, as if it were reading his mind, it yawned and stretched.

"Oh, look at him yawn!" Sherita said.

"Her. He's a her," Jerry corrected.

"Is she your kitten, Jerry? Can I hold her?"

"You can hold her. But she's not my kitten. I mean, she would be but pets aren't allowed in my building. I was hoping you could keep her."

He looked at Mrs. Thomas. She was smiling at the kitten but she still didn't say anything.

"She's no trouble. She uses a box and she doesn't eat much. She even likes being washed. She needs fattening up. She was real skinny when I found her." Jerry told them how he had saved her from the boys. "Those boys would have killed her," he finished.

Sherita picked up the kitten. She cuddled it

under her chin. The kitten reached up with a soft paw and patted Sherita's cheek.

"You don't have to walk her or anything like that," Jerry pointed out. "She's a real good kitten. I'll help you make a litter box. I already know how. And . . ."

The kitten batted at the ladybug on one of Sherita's pigtails.

". . . and she'd be real good company for Sherita after school."

Mrs. Thomas laughed. "Okay, Jerry, okay. You don't have to sell me the kitten. She's already sold herself. And I think you are a hero for bringing her to Sherita," she added softly.

"Um, what are you going to name her?" he asked Sherita.

"Gracie. I'm going to call her Gracie."

"Why Gracie?" Jerry asked.

"Because she's gray, silly."

CHAPTER 15

Jerry sniffed the air as he ran home from school. It smelled funny, sort of frosted. The sky was a strange sort of paper white with a brighter light behind it, like a Japanese lantern. Jerry sent a can spinning ahead of him. It was a fat tin can that had probably once held beans or corn.

He didn't have to worry about Sherita holding him up anymore. Since she'd gotten Gracie she only called him up at night sometimes to talk. She reported every little thing Gracie did. The time she got tangled up in Sherita's hair ribbons. The time she ran from the vacuum cleaner and Sherita couldn't find her for almost an hour. Jerry bet he could write a book about Gracie.

The can shot across the last street. Jerry was glad to be home. He wished those clouds would go away. He was sure they meant rain or snow. Either way they meant no soccer unless they held off for another two hours.

But to his mother, the clouds were the same as snow or rain. "Don't go to the playground today, Jerry," she told him.

"Jeeps, Mom, why not?"

"Because it's either going to snow or rain."

"Not for a while," he protested.

"Jerry."

"Okay, Mom." Jerry hung up and turned on the TV. A cartoon about a pink mouse was on. All the other mice beat it up until it put on its magic cape. Then it became a super mouse that could do anything. Jerry yawned. It was a boring cartoon. His feet itched to run and kick a ball.

It was cold in the apartment. Jerry checked the heat. It was on and the thermostat was on its usual setting. Jerry wondered why he still felt cold. It must be the strange white light coming in through the windows. He changed the channel and found Dr. Monroe in a lab with Dr. James Turner. Dr.

Turner was wearing a long black cape. "I have longed to tell you . . ." he said as he took a step toward Dr. Monroe.

"Yuck," Jerry thought. "Mr. Feeney's favorite program."

Jerry switched again to the educational channel. A nature program about the American desert was on. A snake slithered across the TV screen.

That was better. Jerry sprawled on the sofa. The desert made the room seem a little warmer, but not much.

Jerry watched a sidewinder sidle through the sand. Yucko. Suddenly, dazzling silver light shot through the room. Jerry jumped. It must have been a transformer blowing out somewhere, he thought.

Next a beaded Gila monster oozed along the TV screen. It gave Jerry the creeps. He shivered.

Light flashed at the window. This time Jerry caught a glimpse of the quicksilver, root-shaped light. It was lightning. A drumroll of thunder confirmed it.

Jerry wasn't afraid of thunder and lightning. But the next flash lit up an eerie scene outside his window. Instead of rain, he saw jillions of snowflakes falling silently from the heavy clouds. Jerry ran to the window. The ground was already covered with white. It must have been snowing silently ever since he'd come home.

But snow and lightning? Jerry had never heard of it happening at the same time.

He pulled the curtains together and turned on a lamp. That was better, he thought. But a minute later there was a giant flash and a deafening roar. Both the TV and the lamp went out with a loud snap.

Jerry opened the curtains and stared out of the window. A thick curtain of snow hung from the dull white sky. Snow iced the ledges and window-sills of the apartment building across the street and whitened the rooftops almost to the peaks. There was no color anywhere. The red stop sign at the corner was whited out. The neon lights had been blown out. The world from his window was all gray, black, and white. Jerry thought it looked as though some monster had sucked all the color out of the world. Every few seconds lightning streaked the sky with silver.

It was the scariest, most beautiful sight Jerry had ever seen.

He thought of Sherita. He bet she was scared with the lights out and the weather gone crazy. He wondered why she didn't call him. He sort of wished she would. Maybe he should call her. He wasn't scared, but he wouldn't mind talking to somebody himself.

He dialed her number.

"Hi, Sherita, this is Jerry."

"Hi, Jerry."

There was a pause. Then Jerry said, "Did you look outside?"

"Yes. It's snowing and lightning," she said matter-of-factly. She didn't seem a bit afraid. "I thought it was supposed to rain when it lightninged."

"I thought so, too. It sure is weird weather. Um, Sherita, you're not scared, are you?"

"No. Are you?"

Jerry thought about it. He had been. A little. He wasn't now. But he didn't want to hang up yet. "No. I'm not scared. What are you doing?"

"I'm sitting in a chair with Gracie. We've been eating cookies and I'm reading a story to her. Would you like to hear it?"

"Uh, yeah, I guess so."

"Okay. It's called *Snowbear.* Once upon a time there was a little bear who didn't want to hibernate like all the other bears. 'Why do I have to sleep all winter in a moldy old cave? It's boring. Why can't I stay up and play in the snow?' he asked." Sherita read the little bear's part in a high little voice.

" 'Because you're a bear and bears hibernate all winter,' said his father." She made the father's voice gruff.

" 'Go to sleep, son,' said his mother." Sherita read the mother's voice in her own normal voice.

"When his parents began to snore, he tiptoed out of the cave. Snowflakes fell on the little bear. . . ." Jerry's thoughts began to wander.

"Suddenly there was a loud rumbling, growling sound." Sherita made a low growl and went on reading. "The little bear stopped making a snowball. 'What was that?' he asked his friend the fox."

" 'It was your stomach growling.' "

Jerry laughed. She sounded so funny growling. She didn't seem to be afraid of bears anymore. He wondered if she had bear barrettes on her braids.

"Soon the little bear was snoring, too, and he slept soundly all winter long. The end. Did you like that story, Jerry?"

He did but he was glad his friends couldn't see him listening to a second grader reading a baby book to him over the telephone. "I liked the special effects best," he said.

"The what?"

"Your growling. And that reminds me, I'm hungry, too. And I can't hibernate because I have to study spelling."

"Gracie wants to tell you good-bye. 'Bye, Jerry,'" said a little voice that was supposed to sound like a cat voice.

"Um, bye, Gracie." Jerry hung up and looked out the window. It was still snowing, but the thunder had dwindled to a distant rumble and the lightning was fainter. But the power was still off and it was getting dark. He couldn't watch TV.

Without the TV on, the apartment seemed colder. Jerry put his jacket back on and thought of Mr. Feeney. He probably had on at least three or four coats and several blankets and quilts with only his eyes uncovered so he could watch his programs. Then he remembered that the power was off. Mr. Feeney couldn't watch TV. Jerry wondered what he was doing without his programs.

Jerry thought maybe he should call him. But Mr. Feeney had a telephone. He could call somebody if he wanted to. But he wouldn't, because he wouldn't want to spend the money on a call. Jerry

121

knew he had to do it. He opened the phone book.

Jerry dialed the number. Mr. Feeney picked it up in the middle of the first ring. "Hello? Who's this?"

"It's Jerry, Mr. Feeney. You remember, Jerry Johnson?"

"Oh, yes, I remember. How are you?"

"I'm fine, Mr. Feeney."

"Did you find a home for the cat?"

"I sure did." Jerry told him about Sherita.

"I'm glad to hear it."

There was a pause. Then Jerry said, "Um, Mr. Feeney, is your TV out?"

"It sure is," Mr. Feeney said. "It went off right at the end of 'Hospital Hearts,' just as Dr. Monroe discovered an electronic bug in her stethoscope. I can't wait to find out who put it there."

"I bet it was Arlene Alewine," Jerry said.

"Why would she do that?"

"To get something bad on Dr. Monroe because she wants Michael."

"No, Michael disappeared last week. I think it was his ex-wife Carlotta."

They discussed who might have done it and why. Then Jerry said, "I guess I better hang up now, Mr. Feeney. Um, would you like to go to a soccer game with my dad and me sometime?"

There was a silence. Then Mr. Feeney said, "A soccer game?"

"Yeah. We go on Saturdays when my dad is here." Jerry was beginning to think he'd made Mr. Feeney mad or something.

Jerry waited while Mr. Feeney had a coughing spell. He wondered if Mr. Feeney had on the scarves that made him look like a turtle. "A soccer game, then?"

"Yes, sir."

Mr. Feeney blew his nose. Jerry wondered if he were laughing or crying or having an allergic reaction. He waited politely.

Finally Mr. Feeney said, "Well, I believe I'd like that, Jerry. I do believe I would, weather permitting."

"Okay, Mr. Feeney. See you then."

"Yes, Jerry. I will see you then. Thank you, son."

Jerry hung up. Why had he done that? Mr. Feeney was the last person he wanted to go to a soccer game with. Mr. Feeney probably didn't even like soccer. But he'd sounded like he really wanted to go. Or that he was glad he had been asked. Maybe that was it.

Jerry's mom would probably be home soon. Jerry wondered what they would have for supper since they couldn't use the stove. He hoped she wouldn't decide on salad. Maybe she would order out for pizza. He wondered if Pizza Palace would deliver with all the snow in the streets. Maybe they could heat a can of Sloppy Joe over a candle. Or would it take more than one candle?

He bet even Joel didn't know the answer to that. Jerry would tell him tomorrow at school. But maybe there wouldn't be any school. Maybe everybody would have to stay home. The playground would be piled with snow. Jerry thought about all the things he and his friends could do in the snow. They could build a giant snow fort. They could build the biggest snow fort in the neighborhood, or even the world.